A Toxic Assault

To Blaine

Enjoy the read!

Also by Ted Simon

The Faithless

A Toxic Assault

Ted Simon

iUniverse, Inc.
Bloomington

A Toxic Assault

Copyright © 2010, 2011 by Ted Simon.

All rights reserved. No part of this book may be used or reproduced by any means, graphic, electronic, or mechanical, including photocopying, recording, taping or by any information storage retrieval system without the written permission of the publisher except in the case of brief quotations embodied in critical articles and reviews.

This is a work of fiction. All of the characters, names, incidents, organizations, and dialogue in this novel are either the products of the author's imagination or are used fictitiously.

iUniverse books may be ordered through booksellers or by contacting:

iUniverse
1663 Liberty Drive
Bloomington, IN 47403
www.iuniverse.com
1-800-Authors (1-800-288-4677)

Because of the dynamic nature of the Internet, any web addresses or links contained in this book may have changed since publication and may no longer be valid. The views expressed in this work are solely those of the author and do not necessarily reflect the views of the publisher, and the publisher hereby disclaims any responsibility for them.

Any people depicted in stock imagery provided by Thinkstock are models, and such images are being used for illustrative purposes only.
Certain stock imagery © Thinkstock.

ISBN: 978-1-4620-6281-2 (sc)
ISBN: 978-1-4620-6283-6 (hc)
ISBN: 978-1-4620-6282-9 (ebk)

Printed in the United States of America

iUniverse rev. date: 11/30/2011

Contents

PART I

Chapter 1: Alexa Loves a Pirate 1
Chapter 2: Poisoned How? 6
Chapter 3: Instead of a Funeral 12
Chapter 4: Hatred Starts Young..16
Chapter 5: Death at the Landfill 21
Chapter 6: Bud Follows a Lead..28
Chapter 7: Bad News at the Tabernacle 32
Chapter 8: Alexa Grieves 37
Chapter 9: Trip to the Foundry 39
Chapter 10: Jimmy Ray..44
Chapter 11: She Does Like Me..47
Chapter 12: Alexa's Rising Star..49

PART II

Chapter 13: A Prophet Arrives 59
Chapter 14: Stakeout 63
Chapter 15: A Serious Meeting 73
Chapter 16: A Prophet Speaks...75
Chapter 17: A Prophet Dreams 83
Chapter 18: First Date..92
Chapter 19: In Black and White..100
Chapter 20: Hate Crimes 102
Chapter 21: The Scientist and the Prophet.............................111
Chapter 22: Lunch Interrupted 114
Chapter 23: The March...118

PART III

Chapter 24: Away!...129
Chapter 25: Not So Simple to Escape..............................137
Chapter 26: Some Steel 140
Chapter 27: A Prophet No More..145
Chapter 28: The Pickle Factory 149
Chapter 29: Reasons to Hate...158
Chapter 30: Choose a Martyr..166
Chapter 31: How It Went Down..169
Chapter 32: Where to, Mister?..177

PART I

She's holding out for true love
Waiting on an answer
Ready for a change
And everywhere she goes
She's just a little bit on the lookout
—James Taylor, 1991

Chapter 1

Alexa Loves a Pirate

Saturday, September 9

Alexa Mason walked into the party without a coat or a purse. Her gray eyes flashed as she surveyed the room. A thin strand of pearls circled her long white neck. Thin-strapped high-heeled sandals showed off her slender legs. She had moussed her short dark hair up into a crown. Men stared as she glided across the room in her slinky black mini-dress.

The party host was a wealthy friend of the mayor. His home was a large, old house on Peachtree Circle in Ansley Park. The ornate chair rails and crown moldings in the living room had been refinished. The wallpaper was expensive. The paintings on the walls were originals. The party spread itself over the fifteen or so rooms in the downstairs of the house.

Alexa had met the host only once. She had been invited because she knew the mayor. The party was political—an informal kickoff for the heavy-lifting portion of the mayor's upcoming re-election campaign.

Alexa found the bar and took the champagne proffered by the bartender. Their fingers met, and she winked at him. He smiled at her and mouthed the question, "Later?"

Alexa's answer was a laugh that tinkled across the bar and through the room like the sound of the imported Venetian glass wind chimes on the porch outside.

Although it was just a week after Labor Day, still early September, the evening was cool and pleasant, and a group of partygoers enjoyed the deck in back of the house.

"... so it's not that the people who get caught getting workman's comp when they're able-bodied are bad people, it's just well, they're not hurting that bad anymore, they're at home, and the chores are piling up around the house." A tall dark-haired man in a blue suit was speaking to a slender man with sandy hair and a tall African American man with chiseled features.

"Their injury, if they really had an injury in the first place," blue suit continued, "doesn't feel that bad. That's when they get caught."

"Insurance fraud? Workman's comp?" Alexa asked him.

"You got it. You in the detective bidnez too?"

"I'm in the environmental business," Alexa told the man.

"Consultant?"

Alexa nodded yes.

"Chuck, I was wondering one thing," said the sandy-haired man. "What happens to these guys when they go back to work? Does anyone believe anything they say ever again?"

"Don't know, Bud," said the blue-suited man. "The advice I give is not to lie. Workman's comp fraud amounts to millions a year, and the insurance companies figure it's the same as stealing."

"When I was in the fire department, there were a few guys like that. Took more time off than they really needed," said the black man. He was muscular and fit with chiseled cheekbones below watchful intelligent eyes. His skin was the color of a cup of strong French Roast. He had no jewelry save a Rolex Oyster on his left wrist.

The black man shrugged and nodded.

"I'm forgetting my manners," said blue suit. "I'm Chuck Porter and do some detective work from time to time. You are?"

"Alexa Mason. I've got my own company. We do some work for the city. It's called AMM Services. We do environmental work, just about everything involved with that. Soil and water samples, contract for lab work. Even figure out cleanup strategies."

"This is Jack Williams." Chuck gestured toward the black man. "He probably heard of you because he's the mayor's environmental guy." Alexa shook Jack's hand, noting the firm pressure of his large hand and how it seemed to swallow up hers.

"This is Bud Prior." Chuck motioned toward the sandy-haired man. His dark-blond hair was overly long in front and hung toward his eyes. He was slender and fit-looking without being overly muscular.

"Bud is a cop," said Chuck. "FBI now? Is that right?"

"That's right," said Bud as he shook Alexa's hand. His hand was warm and dry and smaller than Jack Williams's hand. Her hand fit into his so that the webbing between her thumb and index finger fit against Bud's palm. The tips of her fingers lay against his wrist. The handshake felt really good, and she immediately liked Bud. Their eyes met, and Bud smiled at her.

Cops can be pirates too, she thought. *Bud is a nice-looking man.*

After a moment, Chuck turned to Alexa.

"I'm interested in the environmental business," he said. "What's your company again, please?"

"AMM Services. We're small. We have a contract with the state that's our bread and butter. We also do some work for the city."

"You got a card?"

Alexa grinned and showed Chuck her empty hands.

"A purse didn't go with this outfit. AMM Services. I'm in the phone book. Gimme a call and we can talk about it." Her musical laughter turned heads again as it chimed through the night.

"I do need help with something, and I will be calling you," said Chuck.

Alexa cruised back to the bar. As she was getting another glass of champagne, she felt a hand on her arm. It was the dark-skinned man, Jack Williams.

"I'm Jack Williams," he said.

"I remember you, Jack Williams," she said and laughed. "You remember me as well?"

"Alexa Mason. It was just a few minutes ago, and besides, I'm not about to forget a woman who laughs like you do."

This guy Jack doesn't waste any time, she thought. "Are you liking your job with the mayor, Jack, if you don't mind my asking?"

"I do like it so far, but I haven't had the job very long." He looked sheepish. "There was a huge pile of paper on the desk when I got there. Now it's only a little less huge."

"Well, when you get to it, you'll see a report I did last year on the Seitzman's Foundry site. No rush. It won't be that interesting. Tell me about your injury; it sounds dangerous."

"Well, I almost got taken out by a falling beam in a burning building. It just brushed me—or I might not be here."

Alexa responded with a sharp inhalation. She was a sucker for smart men who lived on the edge.

The two grinned at each other again.

"That sounds really dangerous," said Alexa.

"Well . . . yeah, it was," he answered in a self-deprecating way.

Alexa decided right then that if Jack asked, she would leave the party with him.

What was undeniable was that she wanted a man, a strong man—a man with his needs tattooed on his soul. She wanted the dark smell of her pirate sharp in her nostrils and the feel of his psyche greedily wrapping around her own as their bodies entwined.

"Jack, would you take me dancing?" Alexa asked him with a smile, but admonishing herself to take it slow.

When they got to Jack's car, he held the door for her.

When he got in, Jack paused a moment before starting his car.

"Where to, mister?" she asked him and laughed.

"You'll see," Jack told her.

But as they drove away, Alexa found herself thinking of Bud Prior's warm dry handshake and the way he smiled at her.

They went to Backstreet, a late-night bar in Midtown.

Jack was dancing wildly. His sweat-streaked face shone darkly in the strobe lights. They danced together for four songs until, breathless, she leaned in to hug him, catching the dark and tantalizing odor of his sweat mixed with aftershave.

"Jack, I'm hot. I need to catch my breath."

"Get you somethin' to drink as well," Jack whispered in her ear.

Backstreet had a mezzanine where customers could sit and watch the dance floor below.

Jack led Alexa to a table and left her there. He returned with two beers. The music was too loud for anything but the briefest conversation. They drank, smiled at each other.

Dancing until the heat and energy of the dance floor became too much and then cooling off upstairs with a beer became a pattern they repeated twice more. Then, two songs later, Alexa clung to Jack and whispered in his ear.

"Let's go. I'm getting tired of this place."

Jack led her to his black BMW in the parking lot. When they were inside, she leaned over and kissed him. Jack held her face.

"I love your skin," she told him as she touched his cheek. "So smooth and dark, like polished wood—and you're dangerous, you're a pirate."

Jack smiled at her and kissed her again.

"But I want to go slow," she told him with a lump in her throat.

Chapter 2

Poisoned How?

Monday, September 11

Chuck Porter called early that morning. Alexa nodded to Karyn, her receptionist, and took the call in her office.

Chuck made small talk for a moment.

"So what's up?" Alexa asked him.

"I can't give you details on the phone. Why don't you come over here?"

Alexa rolled her eyes.

"Well, I am curious," Alexa told him and agreed to meet. He gave directions. Alexa told Karyn where she would be.

"Alexa, I do a little pro bono work for some of the churches," Chuck told her when they were seated in his office. "I came upon this situation. I've got a mother of twins. One of them is okay, but the other's got something wrong with him. I'm stumped. I've had two other scientists draw a blank. Maybe it's something environmental. That's why I was interested in you."

Chuck scrubbed his face with his hands.

"Alexa, I'm out of my depth on the medical part."

"So far I'm interested," said Alexa.

"The timing is odd," said Chuck. "The kid started to have problems when their church started up a day care center with a playground this summer. The one kid was staying in day care after school. The mother said she started noticing problems about a week after school started."

"What sort of problems?" Alexa probed.

"Well, like I say, they're twins, a boy and girl. She noticed a change in the one that spent time at the day care center—the boy. Started doing poorly in school, ill tempered, couldn't seem to concentrate on anything. Before this summer, he was a model student."

"Any other parents notice or say anything about their kids?"

"Nope."

"So this one mother might be just a crackpot?" Alexa remained skeptical.

"I don't think so," Chuck told her. "Because of their being twins, the mother notices differences in their behavior."

"I take it she's pulled both kids out of day care."

"She has, but nobody else has moved their kids out," said Chuck. "The church is the Summerhill Primitive Missionary Baptist Tabernacle over near Turner Field. Jack Williams grew up in that neighborhood.

"I got the mother coming in shortly, Alexa," Chuck continued. "We'll go easy on her so she doesn't feel like she's being ganged up on. She's older and pretty mistrustful of white people. You understand?"

Alexa nodded.

They talked for a few more minutes until the bell rang, and Chuck brought in a small black woman in a shapeless cotton dress of faded blue.

"Ms. Tohler, this is Alexa Mason. She's helping me with your problem. Would you mind answering a few of her questions?"

"Sure I will." The woman smiled and held out her hand to Alexa.

"Ms. Tohler," began Alexa when they were seated again, "you have two children, right? Twins?"

"That's right. My boy is sick."

"Tell me what you noticed."

"Well, Marcia, she be my gal. She be fine, but she didn't stay at day care. She be over with her friends. She only be at day care for about two or three days at the beginning of school.

"My boy be called DeMario. He be at daycare every day. He stop paying attention in school this fall. Both of them only be seven year old. DeMario don't mind me no more. He quit doing chores less'n I fuss at him, and he been in two fights since school start."

"Ms. Tohler, is he restless? Does he complain about being tired?"

"He real restless all the time, and he do complain about being tired. I don't know what to do about it. He was fine last school year in first grade. It's just since he's been in the day care."

"Ms. Tohler, did uh . . . Marcia go to the same school as DeMario last year?"

"Sure she did. They both in second grade this year. I got me a job working for Georgia State University in maintenance. This day care center in the church be so much better than the one at the university I use last year. It also be close to my house. I likes Reverend Watkins, but I be worried about my kids. I mean, if DeMario don't do well in school . . ."

Alexa watched as the woman started to cry softly. Education was the most certain ticket out of the poverty of the Summerhill neighborhood.

Alexa pulled a tissue from her purse and handed it to the woman.

"Ms. Tohler, I understand your worries. I want you to know the most important thing right now is to get DeMario the help he needs."

Without the woman's trust, Alexa realized, anything else would be moot.

They made plans for Alexa to visit that afternoon.

Alice Tohler and her two children lived in a small bungalow on Spruill Street in Summerhill, about a half-mile northeast of Turner Field. The house needed painting, and several of the boards on the front porch were cracked.

The door opened before Alexa could knock, and Ms. Tohler ushered Alexa into the tiny living room.

A young boy was seated on the floor, playing Nintendo, stabbing at the controls with his thumbs.

"This be DeMario. Stand up and say hello to Ms. Mason," she chided her son, whose attention was concentrated on the television.

The boy was small and dark skinned. He wore a pair of Nike high tops, a pair of shorts, and a Michael Jordan T-shirt.

"Wanna know what they call me in school?" said the boy.

"What do they call you?" Alexa smiled at him.

"Super Mario."

"I see. What should I call you?"

"You can call me Super Mario too."

"How about just Mario?" Alexa felt she might start laughing if she addressed the cute little boy as Super Mario. There was nothing obvious wrong with him so far.

"Mario's okay," he said.

"Do you know why I'm here, Mario?"

"No, and I don't care. I want to get back to my game."

"It's important. Your mom said you've been acting, well . . . different since school started."

"Mario ain't no diff'ent," he said angrily. "My momma be worryin' 'bout my grades in school. Them teachers be teachin' me, then I be learnin'."

The boy yawned deeply.

"Mario, I've got to do some tests on you. First, I've got to look at your gums. Come over by the window, please?"

The boy walked over to Alexa. She pulled on a pair of latex gloves and pushed back his upper lip. In the light coming through the thin curtain, she saw clearly a dark line on his gums near his teeth. Then the boy twisted his head away from her.

Alexa knew the line on his gums, his poor performance in school, his listlessness, and his belligerence could all be caused by lead poisoning.

"I've got to do one more thing, Mario—take some of your blood."

"I ain't gonna be stuck wi' no needle."

"I really need some blood, Mario, to make sure you're okay."

Alexa reached into her bag for a Vacutainer. When she turned around, DeMario's fist crashed squarely into her cheekbone. Alexa went down hard, and her head was ringing.

Her cheekbone stung, and she could feel the anger rising hot inside her. She touched her cheek and felt sticky wetness. Her recognition of the anger and hate in her thoughts and the gulf separating her from DeMario somehow calmed her.

Alexa's chest heaved. She took several deep breaths, willing her agitation to subside.

I've got to get some blood from him, she thought. *I'm pretty sure the kid's been lead poisoned, and I need hard evidence of that.*

She got slowly to her feet and wiped the blood from her cheek with a tissue. DeMario was not in sight.

"Mrs. Tohler," Alexa called. "I need some help."

The woman came in, a puzzled look on her face.

"I tried to take some blood from him. He didn't like it." Alexa pulled the blood-stained tissue away from her face and held it out.

"Now you see what I mean," said Mrs. Tohler. "It don't do no good giving the boy a whippin' neither. I done tried that, and he be just as bad when it's over."

"Ms. Tohler, I need some blood to be certain what's wrong with DeMario. I can get the blood tested within a day, and then we'll know if he needs a doctor."

"A doctor?"

"That's right, Ms. Tohler. It's important not to wait. Otherwise, the changes could be permanent. Where did he go?"

"I fetch him for you."

She came back a few minutes later, leading the boy by his ear.

"You apologize to Ms. Mason. She told me what you done."

"Sorry," whined Mario. His eyes flashed at Alexa with hostility.

The two women sat down on either side of DeMario on the threadbare couch. Alexa held his arm and slipped the needle gently into a vein.

"Three more things, Ms. Tohler."

"Nooooo," wailed DeMario.

"Don't worry. Nothing else from you."

"Git on, boy," said his mother. "What else?" she asked Alexa when the boy had fled the room.

"I need a sample of his sister's blood. I need a sample of your water, and I need to check for lead in the paint on the walls. Is there a faucet you haven't used today?"

"You can take the water from the bathroom the children use."

Alice Tohler led Alexa into a bathroom near the back of the house. Alexa took a sample of the tap water that first came out when she turned the cold water spigot.

Ms. Tohler called Marcia into the room. She was dark skinned like here brother, and her hair was done up in myriad tiny corn rows. Unlike her brother, she held out her arm to Alexa and submitted to the bloodletting without a cry or whimper. Alexa also checked her gums—no dark line.

"The only other thing is to x-ray your walls to see if they have any lead paint. I've got a machine to do that in my car. I'll get it."

Wednesday, September 13

The lab put a rush on the analysis of DeMario Tohler's blood. Alexa had the results of all the tests. There were barely detectable levels of lead in the water and none in the paint on the walls. These were obviously not the source of the lead in DeMario's blood, and the level in his blood was high enough to constitute a medical emergency. But, curiously, Marcia's blood was clean.

As Alexa drove back to Summerhill to break the news to Mrs. Tohler, she wondered where the boy could have been exposed.

"I don't think his blood lead has been this high for very long, and it's good we found this so soon, but DeMario's going to have to go to the hospital right now."

"Good thing I got health care!"

"Grady is the best hospital to deal with this, Ms. Tohler. Let's get DeMario into treatment, and we'll talk at the hospital. I'll drive both of you over there now."

Alexa was able to shepherd the boy through admissions, and when he was with the doctor, she took Ms. Tohler over to the corner of the room.

"Ms. Tohler, this case is very curious. Usually, when we see children with this problem, they got poisoned at home. But your home has no lead. I'm at somewhat of a loss to know where DeMario could have come in contact with that much lead. Marcia has almost no lead in her blood. That also indicates that your home is not the source. Exactly where has DeMario been?"

"You mean without his sister?"

"Yes."

"He go to the day care at the church after school, while Marcia go to singing lessons. Marcia doesn't go to the day care. It's what I told Mr. Chuck. I think it might be the day care."

The whole thing was pretty sad for DeMario. Lead poisoning from a day care center? Alexa wondered if anything could be more awful.

Chapter 3

Instead of a Funeral

Friday, September 15

Six months ago, Sergeant Bud Prior had been a homicide detective in the Atlanta Police Department. He had asked APD for a temporary detail with the FBI to investigate hate crimes, and the request had been granted. He was hoping that if he played his cards right, a federal job might open up for him.

Jack Williams had not shown up to work since Tuesday morning. The mayor's office had called the Atlanta Police Department, and they had referred it to the FBI. Because Williams was black and prominent, the thinking at APD was that his disappearance could possibly be a hate crime.

At the FBI, Bud was partnered with Agent Roscoe Harriman, a tall stocky black man who had been with the FBI for almost thirty years and was looking to retire soon. Bud hoped to learn a lot from Roscoe.

Bud walked down the hall of the FBI offices in the Richard Russell Federal Building. Roscoe's door was open. He looked up as Bud walked in.

"Roscoe, you seen this about Jack Williams? You know, the mayor's aide. Hasn't shown up for work for a few days."

"I was looking into that too, Bud. It doesn't make sense. Williams grew up in the Summerhill neighborhood, which is pretty marginal. Got a full ride at Morehouse, then he went to Emory Law School. Started in private practice at a big downtown firm, but he only lasted a year. Then he went to work for the EPA regional office here in town. He moved on from there to the mayor's office. He did some pro bono on that death penalty stuff a couple of years ago."

"How do you know so much, Roscoe?"

"Mayor's office faxed me his résumé. Was about a year ago, the mayor picked him to be the environmental boss in city hall."

"Pretty exceptional guy!"

"Yeah, and he's always stayed in touch with his roots. I never met him, but I figure he was pretty ambitious—politics and all. He was just biding his time."

"So we're looking into this?"

"I got a feeling this is our case, Bud. We should start in his old neighborhood."

Sunday, September 17

The Reverend Rufus B. Watkins surveyed his meager flock gathered at the Summerhill Primitive Missionary Baptist Tabernacle. Less than one hundred hands held up hymnals, and less than one hundred eyes scanned the music on the page.

The time had come for the sermon, but the Reverend Watkins hesitated. The congregation was expecting him to talk about Jack Williams's disappearance. Watkins did not want to give the impression that he or the church had given Jack up for dead.

The Reverend Watkins shuffled through his notes. The congregation stared up at him expectantly. He cleared his throat and began.

"Brothers and sisters, we come together this Sunday morn to think and ponder what the Lord means for us to do." His sonorous ringing baritone was solemn, fitting for a man of God. "We are not here to mourn our brother, but to pray for his safe passage."

A chant, sounding like a lament, rose from the congregation.

"I don't believe he be gone, brothers and sisters. He be calling us in a day or so."

A chorus of "That's right" and "Amen" arose from the congregation. One of the women in the front row fanned herself and stared at Reverend Watkins with skepticism. He waited for the congregation to be silent before he continued.

"We can do nothing now, brothers and sisters. We gonna just keep right with God. The church gonna help you from now on. What, brothers and sisters, be the great joy and great worry in your life? Your children? Am I right? That's what Jack would say if he was here.

"The church gonna be taking better care of your children. We gonna grow that day care center that my lovely wife Hattie runs during the week so you folks can go to work and not worry about your precious children.

"The Lord helps those that help themselves. We gonna help ourselves, and then see what the Lord gonna do for us and for Jack Williams."

Bud Prior and Roscoe Harriman stood respectfully at the back of the church and listened to Watkins hold forth.

The Reverend had finished his sermon and was giving the benediction.

"Oh, Lord, we pray for the deliverance of one of our own," Watkins continued. "Brother Jack Williams be not just a man trying to get through his life. He be a man who want to make a difference, who strongly believed that he should leave the world better than he found it.

"We know him—the way he helped build the church day care center, the way he raised funds. We miss him something terrible."

Special Agent Roscoe Harriman leaned toward Bud and whispered.

"They're acting like he's more than just missing."

"Roscoe," Bud whispered back, "they've already given him up for dead."

They listened as the preacher continued to speak, extolling Jack Williams's virtues and accomplishments.

"Man," whispered Bud, "Jack Williams sounds like he walks on water."

The Reverend Watkins was winding up. His words were poignant, like a eulogy. Bud and Roscoe quietly left the church when the service was over and stood respectfully in the September sunlight at the edge of the parking lot.

"So, last Monday, Jack doesn't show up at work, doesn't show up anywhere," said Bud. He looked to Roscoe for confirmation.

"That's about the size of it," said Roscoe and shrugged, his eyes blank.

"We'll find his body somewhere," Bud said quietly. "The guy had too much going for him just to quit."

Several of the women were crying as they got in their cars parked next to the small church. Evidently, they had reached the same conclusion.

There was a playground behind the church building and off to one side. The swings and seesaws looked new. The playground was in a low spot, and the recently added fill dirt was a coppery reddish-brown color. The rest of the church seemed shabby.

Bud hoped they would be done soon so he could pick up his eight-year-old son, Christopher, from the sitter. Bud was a single parent. His wife had died from leukemia a couple of years after Christopher was born. Bud knew he should be looking to get married again—to provide the boy a mother. Christopher had asked about his mother only once, and Bud didn't think the boy remembered her.

A wife would make my life easier, he thought as he checked his watch. *I wouldn't have to clock watch all the time to make sure I get to school or day care on time to pick Christopher up, but the thought of another woman in my life still scares me.*

"Let's talk to the Reverend before he leaves," said Roscoe, interrupting Bud's reverie.

The Reverend Rufus B. Watkins was a large man both in height and girth. He was sweating, and his dark skin shone.

"Reverend Watkins, I'm Roscoe Harriman. You remember me?"

"I sure do," said the Reverend, pumping Roscoe's hand.

"This is Bud Prior. He works with me. Jack Williams isn't one to turn up missing. Did you know him well?"

"I didn't know him except within the church. He did a lot for the church."

"You know if he had any enemies, anyone who would wish him harm?" asked Bud.

"Jack Williams? Are you kidding?" answered the Reverend immediately. "But working in the mayor's office—well, that be another story. Maybe he made some enemies there."

Bud nodded and wrote on his notepad.

"I hope he still be showing back up," said the Reverend Watkins when Bud looked up. "I ain't give up on him."

The Reverend was right. The mayor's office seemed a more likely place for Williams to have angered someone enough to kill him than this poor tiny church.

Chapter 4

Hatred Starts Young

Monday, September 18

On Monday, there was no more news about Jack Williams. Bud remained at his desk all day doing paperwork.

At 4:30 p.m., Bud drove east on Ponce to pick up Christopher. He got to the after-school care with twenty minutes to spare, and Bud could see the boy was glad to see him from the way Christopher ran to the car. Like his father, Christopher had a slender build and sandy-blond hair.

"Hey, Christopher. Did you have fun today?"

"Sure did, Dad." He was grinning. "I played tetherball most of the afternoon." Then the boy's face clouded a moment.

"What is it, Christopher?"

"Something weird happened this morning. Angela Sellers got in trouble, and I don't know why. Fred Clark pulled her pigtails, and she got really mad."

"Uh-huh," said Bud, indicating to his son to continue.

"Well, she called him a name. One of the teachers heard it and got mad at Angela. I didn't understand. Isn't pulling her pigtails worse than any name-calling?"

Bud smiled, remembering when he had taught Christopher the ancient rhyme about sensitivity to insults.

"What did she call him, Chris?"

"She said he was a dumb nigger."

The after-school program Bud had chosen for Christopher prided itself on diversity and tolerance.

"You know what that means, Christopher?"

"No, Dad."

"You know, just because a person has darker skin than you doesn't make them any different than you."

"Yeah, I know, Dad. You've told me before." The boy was impatient, wanting an explanation.

"She called him a really ugly name for a black person."

"Nigger."

"Yeah. It's a word you want to be really careful with, Christopher."

"I guess so. The teacher who heard it pulled Angela away from the group and off into the corner."

"Christopher, you know those other words you're not supposed to say. Well, 'nigger' is worse than any of those words."

"I don't get it, Daddy," said Christopher. "Why is it so bad?"

"It's the worst thing a white person can call a black person. We've been living here in Atlanta where most people don't act like that. They wouldn't think of calling someone a name like that.

"Christopher, I've always tried to show you that I believe that white people and black people are the same except for their skin color. We're all human beings and you should treat everyone the way you want to be treated."

"I understand, Dad."

When his wife Sandi had died, Bud could not face the emptiness of the house he had shared with his wife. Their house was in Alpharetta, a suburb north of the city. Bud sold quickly, taking a loss, and moved into a small house in Decatur, a quiet in-town neighborhood.

Living in town was better, he felt. The house in Decatur was closer to the orbit of his days, and unlike many in Atlanta, Bud did not feel that he was spending his life in his car. From the house, Bud was within twenty minutes of a good public school, after-school care for Christopher, and his workplace.

"It made me feel bad when I heard Angela," said Christopher. The boy's words were earnest and without guile. Bud felt his heart fill with love.

"Christopher, people learn to hate other people in all kinds of ways. Prejudice is what this is called—hating someone just because of race or religion. Really, prejudice is hating someone just because they're different than you. It's important to judge people by the way they act and not the way they look."

"You told me that before, Dad. So I've been trying to be nice to the younger kids at school. I've been reading to some of the six-year-olds."

"That's great, Christopher. It's so much better to treat people nicely than to be mean."

"I know, Dad."

The Decatur City Schools were, by reputation, excellent. Clearly, Christopher was learning social skills as well as the three R's.

With a lump in his throat, Bud thought of Sandi and then reflected on the few other women who had been in his life and his present loneliness.

"Christopher, we need to go to Trader Joe's on the way home. You've got nothing for breakfast tomorrow."

"You know I love Trader Joe's, Dad. Can we go to Starbucks too?" Bud was a coffee drinker and had begun taking his son to Starbucks as a treat for both of them.

"Sure." He grinned at his son.

Bud shopped at Trader Joe's because he believed the food sold there was generally healthier than what was available at mass-market grocery stores. The store closest to Decatur was in an old but upscale shopping center in Virginia-Highlands.

They walked in, and Bud took a buggy and started down the produce aisle.

"Christopher, you know that chocolate-covered ginger you like? Can you go pick up some of that?" Candy was on the next aisle, and Bud knew his son liked helping him shop rather than just tagging along.

When Bud pushed the buggy into the next aisle, he saw Christopher leaning across a case of frozen items, trying without success to reach the candy.

A slender, pretty, dark-haired woman Bud recognized from somewhere helped Christopher reach the candy.

"Is this what you want?" she asked. It was the woman from the mayor's party.

"Thanks," said Christopher as Bud approached them.

"You're, uh . . . Bud Prior, right?" said Alexa. "I remember from the party."

"I remember you too," said Bud, "but not your name, I'm embarrassed to say."

"Alexa Mason." She reached to shake his hand again. "I'm sorry we didn't get a chance to talk more at the party."

"It seems like a big coincidence running into you again, Alexa. Atlanta's a big town."

"You shop here much, Bud?"

"Once a week. You?"

"I just live around the corner toward Virginia-Highlands, so I'm here a lot. This is your son?"

Bud nodded. "Christopher, say hello to Ms. Mason."

The boy proffered his hand, and Alexa shook it.

"I'd rather you called me Alexa," she said. "You have a good handshake, Christopher. Just like your dad's. I can see he's done a great job to raise a nice young man like you."

Both father and son blushed at the compliment.

"Alexa, one of our rituals is to hit Starbucks after the grocery store. Would you care to join us?"

"I'd love to. I'll finish my shopping and meet you there."

"She was really nice, Dad," said Christopher when they had moved onto the next aisle. "I'm glad she'll be at Starbucks." They finished shopping but didn't see Alexa in the store again.

"Do you like her too, Dad?" asked Christopher as they stowed the groceries behind the seat in Bud's truck. "She's really pretty too."

"She does seem really nice," said Bud.

Alexa is way too young for me, thought Bud. *Hardly more than a girl.*

They walked into Starbucks, and Alexa waved to them from a table in the corner of the room.

"I didn't order, just got a table. Most times, it's packed in here."

"Christopher, I know what you want. How about you, Alexa?"

"Decaf latte. No sugar."

Bud went to the counter and ordered their drinks along with a small coffee for himself. He noted that Christopher and Alexa were talking animatedly. When the drinks were done, he carried them back to the table and passed them round.

"How'd you know I like a straw?" asked Alexa.

"Didn't. I just did yours the same as Christopher's."

"It's perfect," she said, her eyes twinkling up at him.

Bud sat down and sipped his coffee.

"At the party, Chuck said you're FBI?"

"Sort of. I'm actually in the Atlanta Police Department, but I'm on loan to the feds. I'd love to try to work it into a federal job. Good benefits and time off." He nodded his head toward Christopher. "I'm the only one raising this boy." He tousled his son's hair.

"That must be tough," said Alexa. "I love children, but I've never had my own. So what do you do for the FBI?"

"I'm in the hate crimes unit right now."

"Doesn't seem like there'd be as much to do as there was a few years ago."

"Alexa, you'd be surprised at what some people do. How about you?"

"I've got my own little business. AMM Services. Environmental work. My office is downtown. I do some work for the state and the city. I don't know where it's going, but I'm enjoying it now. I've only got one employee, and I might just keep it that way. I actually like the work and don't want to spend my time managing people." She laughed again. Bud's heart skipped a beat; she had one of the most beautiful laughs he'd ever heard. Her laugh invited him to know her better; it held the promise of friendship, warmth, a hint of feminine mystery and even love."

"So, Alexa," chimed in Christopher, "do you like the zoo?"

"I do like the zoo. I studied biology in school, and I think animals and everything about them is way cool.

"Dad, can Alexa come to the zoo with us sometime?"

"I'd love to go to the zoo with you," she said before Bud could demur.

Their eyes met, and Bud could again see the twinkle in them. It was impossible not to like her. *At least she knows the baggage I've got*, he thought. *Whoever I end up with has got to have a relationship with Christopher as well as me. Alexa's a ways down that road already.*

"Did you finish your drink, Christopher?" said Bud.

"'Bout half done," the boy answered. "Can we pick a time to go to the zoo now?"

"Not now," Bud told his son, "but I promise we'll go as soon as we can."

"Are you still game?" he asked Alexa.

"Of course, Bud." She took out a card and wrote on it. "Here's all three of my numbers. What a great father you are!"

She stood up to leave, and Bud stood as well. Alexa took a step toward him, stood on tiptoe, and kissed him on the cheek.

Chapter 5

Death at the Landfill

Thursday, September 21

Alexa Mason parked her van in the parking lot of the Cedartown landfill at about 9:30 in the morning. The landfill had operated as a municipal dump for just under fifty years. Puffy cumulus clouds sailed through the sunny blue sky. The landfill appeared as a big mound of reddish earth at the side of the road on the outskirts of town. A construction trailer stood at the landfill entrance. Next to it was a tent and outdoor shower used for decontamination.

Alexa was there to provide independent oversight on some trench sampling. Oversight was a good gig, easy money. All Alexa had to do was watch the sampling procedure, make sure things were done right, and send a memo to that effect once back in the office.

Alexa donned coveralls and hip boots and walked over to the backhoe at the far corner of the landfill. She stared a moment at the man on the backhoe. He was tall and lean, and his movements on the controls were graceful economies.

Alexa saw that his head was shaved when he took off his hard hat to rub his head. The sleeve of his shirt rode up to reveal a tattoo. The man was a little scary looking, but of course Alexa's wild heart, the part of her that craved a pirate, was fascinated.

Fred Smith, the state coordinator, hurried over to her with a map.

"Alexa, glad you were free this morning. I've got a map here. Check it out before we start trenching and see if you agree with the locations. I've only got this crew for today. They're from that lead foundry in Atlanta."

Alexa studied the map.

"Fred, I want to walk the perimeter first. Okay?"

"Anything you say. I want the oversight report to concur with what I did."

Fred turned to the man on the backhoe as Alexa walked away.

"Hold off on any digging, please. Wait until we get back."

"Sure," said the man.

Over in the other corner of the landfill, in an area supposed to be closed, they found some red dirt, newly exposed like a wound.

"Fred, what's up with the digging here? Isn't this part of the landfill closed? New cells are only supposed to go over on the northeast side." She wondered if some midnight dumping had occurred.

"Don't know," said Fred. "Anyway, we gotta get three trench samples. Why don't we take one there? If someone did dump something illegally—well, that's the kind of sample I need. I'll tell the backhoe guy. Man, he's a strange bird. Never speaks. I'm glad he's just filling in today."

Fred walked over to the backhoe and pointed to where Alexa stood. Then he climbed on and rode the backhoe to the spot. He motioned the sample collection team over as the backhoe started to dig. The big bucket bit into the thick clay over the garbage. As the bucket surfaced, black plastic shreds from old garbage bags hung eerily from its teeth. Alexa noted that the clay layer over the landfill cell was less than six inches thick, well below regulation.

The backhoe reversed for another bite, and the ground shook as the big bucket dug into the landfill a second time. The operator dumped the contents of the bucket next to the hole.

"Fred, did you see something in that last load?"

"Stop!" he called out, waving at the backhoe man.

Alexa pulled a shovel from the rear of the backhoe and pushed away clumps of soil and garbage from a dark-skinned hand with a Rolex Oyster on its wrist. The rest of the body remained buried beneath the decaying garbage and red clay cover of the landfill. She stared at the hand a moment in shock and then looked away.

The Cedartown patrolman got out of his unit. He was there by himself. His shoes were well polished, and his dark blue uniform was clean. He frowned as if unhappy to be there.

"Who saw the body first?" he asked.

"I did," said Alexa, "but I haven't seen the whole body. All I saw was a hand—African American."

The patrolman pursed his lips, and the furrows in his brow deepened.

"No one goes back there. I'm calling my sergeant."

The sergeant arrived twenty minutes later.

Alexa watched the two cops stretch yellow crime scene tape across the entrance to the landfill.

"I'm Sergeant Miller," said the older man to Alexa. "You found the body first, right?"

"That's right, Sergeant."

"Someone's obviously gone to some trouble to try and hide this body. I've got the FBI coming. It would be very helpful if you could stick around and talk to them."

"No problem," Alexa told him.

While they were waiting for the FBI, four pickup trucks pulled up and parked on the shoulder outside the landfill. Six Klansmen in hoods and robes got out and began marching up and down at the entrance to the landfill, holding up signs.

"Fred," Alexa said, pointing at the marchers.

"What now?" said Fred. "Jesus H. Christ, this is all I need. I'm supposed to be keeping to a schedule here."

They walked toward the protestors. One of the signs read: Fairness in hiring! Another read: Hire local.

"What are they protesting?" Alexa asked Fred.

"There was a guy who worked here before we closed the landfill. He drove the bulldozer. They said he was a pretty good heavy equipment man. I'd have hired him, but he didn't have forty hours of OSHA HazMat training. There was nothing I could do. Insurance regs say I can't hire someone without the training."

"And the contractor you did hire has African Americans working, right?"

"Yup."

Bud Prior took the call from the Cedartown police.

"Roscoe, we've got a probable murder in Cedartown. Where the heck is that, by the way? Police sergeant who called says there's a pretty active Klan out there and the victim's black. No evidence it's a hate crime, but he's calling us just to be on the safe side."

"I know where it is. I'll drive."

There was a long uphill stretch on the road to the landfill. Ten men wearing white robes with pointed hoods paraded in front of the landfill gate.

"God, I hate Kluckers," said Roscoe, grim-faced. He pulled the flashing light from under the seat and clamped it firmly to the roof of the car. A single blast on the siren scattered the Klansmen.

Bud got out of the car as soon as they parked. Standing over by the dirt path into the landfill were two local cops, another man with a clipboard, and a slender dark-haired woman. It was Alexa Mason.

The two agents ducked under the yellow crime scene tape and walked over to the group.

"I'm Sergeant Miller," said the older cop, extending his hand to Bud and Roscoe. "This is Officer Dalton. Mr. Smith here is the on-scene coordinator from the state environmental people. Ms. Mason here found the body."

"I'm Sergeant Bud Prior and this is Special Agent Roscoe Harriman. Ms. Mason and I have already met," said Bud.

"I'm working as the oversight contractor for the state," Alexa volunteered.

Bud looked at her a moment. Her short dark hair framed her lovely face. Involuntarily, Bud held his breath. He had almost forgotten how beautiful she was.

Bud recalled a former lover—Suzanne, a cop like himself, fatally shot. The attraction he felt toward Alexa Mason reminded him of his jinx, that the women he loved ended up dead.

Bud closed his eyes briefly. When he opened them, she was looking right at him, smiling with twinkling eyes.

"Sergeant Prior is on detail from Atlanta PD," said Roscoe. "Why do you think this is a hate crime, Sergeant Miller?"

"I don't know exactly, Agent Harriman, but someone went to a lot of trouble to hide this body in the landfill. Victim was a black man. Well, you can see there's a pretty active Klan out here in Cedartown."

"Yeah, we noticed," said Roscoe sardonically.

"What're those guys out front protesting?" asked Bud. "Surely not the murder of an African American."

"Naw," said the Sergeant. "When they closed the landfill, they fired the local crew who drove the bulldozer. Crew they brought in for the hazardous waste investigation had some African Americans. It's a labor thing. You know, angry white males."

"Okay," said Bud. "There's not gonna be any work done here until we investigate."

"Sir, please," said the state coordinator, "I got a schedule to keep here to satisfy my management at the state."

"We'll be as quick as we can," said Roscoe. "You think we could see the body?"

"I'll take them," said Alexa. She led Bud and Roscoe to the decontamination tent and handed them coveralls and hip boots.

"Put 'em on," she told them. "It'll save your shoes.

In spite of the clunky hip boots, Bud noticed that Alexa's walk was poised and graceful. Bud and Roscoe followed her through the sticky clay of the landfill cover.

"There it is," she said, pointing to a dark-skinned hand, a Rolex watch on its wrist, protruding from the cuff of a yellow shirt. The rest of the body was buried beneath a pile of dirt and garbage.

"Likely he was killed somewhere else," said Bud. "We'll treat it as a crime scene anyway. Roscoe, where can we get a CSI unit?"

"GBI. I'm calling them."

"Wait," said Alexa, placing her hand on Bud's forearm. "We don't know what's in this landfill. Anyone who wants to move that dirt or clean the body needs a HazMat team."

"It just looks like red Georgia clay," said Bud in disbelief.

"Look, this landfill may become a Superfund site. They've been dumping who knows what here for fifty years."

"Roscoe?" asked Bud.

"I don't want to be responsible for anyone getting hurt. I'll tell the GBI to bring a HazMat team as well." He flipped open his phone.

The HazMat team commandeered the decon tent and moved the body in there. Doc Caldwell, the Fulton County M.E., wore a chemical hazard suit for the preliminary autopsy, which he performed by himself in the decon tent.

"Do you need me anymore?" Alexa asked Bud after the autopsy had begun.

"I don't think so," said Bud.

"It was nice to see you again, Bud." Her eyes twinkled as she smiled. "Even under these circumstances."

"How can we get in touch if we need to, Ms. Mason?" asked Roscoe.

She gave them each a business card.

Bud and Roscoe watched Alexa get into a small blue Toyota and drive away. He and Roscoe leaned against the fender of the government sedan and waited until Doc Caldwell came out of the decon tent.

"I met her at that party for the mayor," Bud volunteered as they waited.

"She likes you," said Roscoe, grinning at him. "An old man like me can tell."

"She's very beautiful," said Bud, "but I'm way too old for her."

They fell silent as Caldwell approached.

"I got his fingerprints," said Doc. "Someone cut his throat, and he bled to death. It was meant to happen. I'd say you got a premeditated murder."

"So, Doc, who is the vic'?" asked Bud.

"Can't tell yet. I have to wait till I get to the office to match the fingerprints."

Bud and Roscoe looked at each other.

"I also found this." Caldwell handed over a business card with a round emblem of a dark cross in a field of white flowers. They looked like lilies. "It was in his shirt pocket."

"You know what this is, Bud?" said Roscoe.

"Not sure," Bud replied.

"It's the sign of the Southern Mystic Knights of the Invisible Empire," Roscoe told him. "Maybe the Klan was involved, or maybe someone wanted us to assume the Klan was involved. Maybe those guys out front are just a setup."

Chapter 6

Bud Follows a Lead

Friday, September 22

After dropping Christopher at school, Bud checked his phone messages at work. Doc Caldwell had left him a voice mail indicating the victim was indeed Jack Williams.

Bud took his own vehicle, a white Mazda pickup, out to Cedartown. He started at the landfill. A group of men in hip boots and hardhats were standing around a construction trailer drinking coffee. Half of them were African American. Bud wondered how they felt about the presence of the Klan yesterday.

"The boss inside?" Bud asked them.

"Go on in," one man told him.

Two men were inside arguing. Bud recognized one of them as Fred Smith, the state coordinator. He didn't know the other man.

"Mr. Smith," said Bud, "I'm Sergeant Bud Prior working with the FBI. I was out here yesterday."

"That's right. I remember. This gentleman is Gray Winters. He's the former operator of the landfill."

"Mr. Winters, I'm Sergeant Bud Prior of the Atlanta Police on detail to the FBI. One thing I was wondering about was the Klan being here yesterday. Why? They're not interested in hazardous waste, are they?"

"It ain't that," said Winters. "I had a man workin' for me 'fore the state took over. Best backhoe an' dozer man I ever seen. Name o' Jimmy Ray Groover. I had to let him go when they closed the landfill. I think maybe Jimmy Ray was in the Klan. Anyway, you see this new crew. They decided to use the ol' D-9 cat that Jimmy Ray drove. Put a nig—" He cleared his throat to hide the inadvertent slur. ". . . a black up on the D-9. Jimmy Ray saw him when he got his last check. I figger that's what the Klan is riled up about. I guess they think we should hire Jimmy Ray instead. Thing is, the company won't touch anyone without HazMat training."

"An' Jimmy Ray didn't have the training?"

"No, we was a municipal landfill and didn't figger we had any hazardous waste here. Now the state says different. Besides, the training's pretty expensive. A thousand dollars."

"So Jimmy Ray had access to the landfill before it was closed."

"That's right. He worked for me for 'bout two years. Like I said, he was the best I ever seen. I told 'em they should give him a job. I told 'em no one drove a D-9 like Jimmy Ray."

"I'd like to talk to Jimmy Ray."

"I got his number."

The loss of his job was a possible motive for Jimmy Ray. His possible Klan connection suggested he might have taken out his anger on the first black man he encountered. His access to the landfill provided him the opportunity to bury the body. He was the best suspect so far. If he hadn't killed Jack Williams, he probably knew who had.

Bud used his cell phone to call Jimmy Ray's number.

"Hello," a woman's voice answered. In the background, Bud could hear a child crying.

"Hello," he said, "I'm Sergeant Bud Prior of the FBI. I'm trying to find Jimmy Ray Groover."

"Jimmy Ray's not in trouble, is he?"

"No, ma'am. I just have a few questions for him. Do you know where he is?"

"I'm his wife, Melanie. He's been goin' to a new job in Atlanta since last Friday. He got up real early this mornin' and left. I guess that's where he is."

"Ms. Groover, could I ask you a few questions? It won't take long."

"I'd rather have Jimmy Ray here," she said.

"I understand, but a little information from you would really help my investigation. I just want to develop some other leads."

"I'm stuck home," she told him. "You'll have to come here. I can't talk long. I got kids to take care of."

"I promise it won't take long. If you'd just tell me where you live?"

Bud parked his truck near the Groover's mobile home. To the left, a rusted out junker car sat up on cinder blocks under a tree. The hood was open, and hanging from a tree above it was a chain pulley for lifting motors. The motor itself was gone.

On the other side of the house were several doghouses inside a wire pen. When Bud got out of his truck, a large brindle pit bull emerged from one of the doghouses and began barking.

Bud knocked on the front door of the mobile home.

"Come round to the back, please!" called a woman's voice from inside.

Behind the mobile home was a large screened porch with a litter of toys and two adult-sized chairs. The back door of the mobile home opened onto the porch, and a pretty blonde woman stepped out.

She was a little plump around the chin. Her hair hung in thick curls around her face. She wore jeans and a loose-fitting shirt. She was barefoot and wore no makeup.

"I'm Melanie Groover. Are you the cop?"

"Sergeant Bud Prior." He showed her his shield.

"You can come in, Sergeant. I'm feeding Kelly. She's one of my twins."

"Thank you, Ms. Groover."

She offered him a chair and went back to spooning strained carrots into Kelly's waiting mouth.

"Ms. Groover, your husband used to work at the landfill, right?"

"That's right. Jimmy Ray told me they closed it down. He didn't say why. He don't talk much when he comes home, Sergeant."

"You said Jimmy Ray had another job in Atlanta?"

"He told me 'bout it the other night. He met a guy who needed a bulldozer man. Jimmy Ray's a good dozer man," she said proudly. "Anyway, he was goin' to Atlanta to see 'bout this job. I don't work, an' somebody's gotta support these two kids. Jimmy Ray's always been a good provider."

"He didn't say where this job was?"

"A foundry with some hazardous waste. Somethin' like that. I told him to be careful and not get hurt. I couldn't hold down a job and raise these two kids."

"You sure he didn't say where the new job was."

"Nope. Jimmy Ray, well, he don't tell me much 'bout his work." She wiped Kelly's mouth with a washcloth.

"Is there anything else, Sergeant?"

"Just one thing, Ms. Groover. Is Jimmy Ray in the Klan?"

She looked at Bud hard, and the spoon with its load of carrots stopped midway between the jar and Kelly's waiting mouth. She put the spoon back in the jar and stared at the floor for a long moment.

"I told him when we got married that I didn't want him hanging around with the Klan. He messed around with those idiots before we was married."

Bud looked at her steadily and waited until she realized she hadn't really answered his question.

"Well . . ." he said.

"I don't know, Sergeant," answered Melanie Groover, "and that's the truth. I sure hope he ain't, but I really don't know."

"You expect him back tonight, don't you, Ms. Groover?"

"I hope so, but with Jimmy Ray, you can't tell."

"I'm going to try to find him wherever he's working in Atlanta. You sure he didn't tell you where it is?"

"I'm sorry, Sergeant. No." Her face fell. "Jimmy Ray's in trouble, isn't he?"

Bud looked at her a moment. "Here's my card, Ms. Groover. Call me whenever you want."

Chapter 7

Bad News at the Tabernacle

Saturday, September 23

Alexa had spent the next two days fretting that the dead man in the landfill was Jack Williams. He wore a Rolex, and she couldn't get the image of the Rolex on the dead man's wrist out of her mind.

She had been trying, whenever she had a free moment, to call Chuck Porter and follow up on what she had done with DeMario Tohler. But Alexa had been unable to reach Chuck. She felt some urgency because she suspected the source of the lead was the day care and other children were at risk.

Even though it was Saturday, she was in her office, finishing the oversight report for the Cedartown Landfill when the phone rang.

"AMM Environmental. Alexa Mason," she answered.

"Alexa? This is Chuck Porter."

"I've tried to call you, Chuck. I need to give you a report on DeMario Tohler. I'm also worried about other children."

"That's what I was calling about, Alexa. I talked to his mother already, and she told me he was in the hospital."

"Yeah, I told them to go to the hospital. DeMario's blood lead was over sixty micrograms per deciliter. He was on his way to permanent brain damage."

"Man, oh, man!" exclaimed Chuck. "I didn't know it was that serious. How would he get lead in his blood?"

"I figured it was most likely from his home, but there's no lead in either the tap water or the paint on the walls. The difference between the two kids is whether they spent time at that church day care. I need to look there next. Can you get me in?"

"No problem, Alexa."

"Chuck, I don't feel right sashaying up to the church and asking if I can take some soil samples. Last time I asked that question, the answer wasn't just no, it was hell no!"

"Don't worry about it, Alexa. I understand. I've got a good relationship with the Reverend Watkins. Look, can you get free now? I'd like to meet you there as soon as possible. Like you said, if the lead is in the day care, well, there's other kids there right now. We've also got to think of them."

"I'm on my way, Chuck."

The Summerhill Primitive Missionary Baptist Tabernacle was locked when they got there. Chuck called and roused the Reverend Watkins from sleep.

"I'm sorry I ain't at the church, Mr. Chuck," Reverend Watkins told them when he arrived. He wore black pants and shoes. A wrinkled white shirt hung outside his pants. His girth remained undisguised by his loose-fitting clothes. Sparse gray whisker stubble dotted his cheeks.

"This is Alexa Mason. Alexa, the Reverend Rufus B. Watkins."

Alexa reached out and shook Watkins's hand.

"Alexa's helping me with the business of DeMario Tohler." He motioned to Alexa to start.

"Reverend Watkins," she said, hesitating a moment to choose her words. "I examined DeMario about ten days ago and discovered that he had been exposed to very high levels of lead."

"Lead?"

"You know, the metal. They used to make car batteries and fishing sinkers out of it. Well, lead damages children's brains and interferes with their ability to learn. I checked DeMario's home and found no sources of lead there. I heard from DeMario's mother that he spent time here at the day care center. I wondered if I could see it."

"Reverend Watkins," said Chuck, "what Alexa wants to do is to ensure that no other children will be harmed the way DeMario was. We know you have nothing but good intentions for the children of Summerhill. We want to make sure those good intentions come to pass."

"No problem, Mr. Chuck," Reverend Watkins answered with a smile.

"Ms. Lexa, right?"

"That's right," she told him.

"I want Hattie's day care to be the best it can be. Hattie's my wife. You do whatever you need to do."

Alexa smiled and cast a relieved glance at Chuck as the Reverend Watkins opened the front door of the church and led them into the day care center. About a dozen children were sitting on mats on the floor quietly reading or coloring. A woman of similar girth to the Reverend sat in the corner watching the children. She raised her eyebrows quizzically when she saw them come in.

"It's okay, Hattie," he told her. "These folks need to check things out. 'Member Ms. Tohler?"

"Oh, right, Rufus," she said.

Alexa had her kit with her and promptly took some water and paint samples.

"The children go outside, don't they?" she asked.

"Sure do. We just built the playground. C'mon with me." The Reverend led Chuck and Alexa out a door and into the bright September sun.

A young woman, her hair done in cornrows, stood in a corner of the playground and watched a dozen more children as they played on the swings and seesaws. The playground was fenced, and the equipment was new. The ground inside the fence had no grass; it was dusty red Georgia clay. The playground land surface was a little higher than the area outside the fence.

That looks like new fill dirt, she thought. *I wonder where it came from.*

"Reverend Watkins, do you know exactly where DeMario liked to play?"

"I can find out for you, Ms. Alexa." He went over and spoke briefly to the young woman, then motioned for Alexa and Chuck to join him.

"This is Yolanda Watson, the aide here at the day care. She stays outside with the children on the playground."

"Ms. Watson," said Alexa, "did DeMario Tohler have a favorite area of the playground?"

"DeMario? He left last week, right?"

"That's right."

"Something about him being sick."

"That's right. Did he have a special place in the playground where he liked to play?"

"He was always on the second swing. That one." Yolanda pointed. A young boy on the second swing swung as high as he could, an expression of glee on his face. His feet scraped the ground, raising a cloud of red dust each time he swung back and forth.

Alexa grinned at him and waited. He saw her and smiled back, trying to swing even higher to show off.

The three of them heard a car pull into the church parking lot and turned to look. A blue Ford Taurus idled and then stopped. Two men got out, one black and one white. It was Bud Prior and his partner Roscoe. Alexa thought it was curious that she kept running into Bud Prior.

The two men walked up to the fence surrounding the playground, and Roscoe motioned to Reverend Watkins to join him.

Alexa shielded her eyes from the sun. As Roscoe talked to the Reverend Watkins, Bud moved a respectful distance away along the fence.

Alexa stared at Bud. He seemed mature and experienced; it showed in the way he carried himself. Nonetheless, his stomach was flat, and his longish sandy hair fell across his forehead in a sexy boyish way.

Alexa felt a sting of attraction for Bud. *I don't know exactly why I like him*, she thought, *but he's a great father to his son, obviously kind. Working for the FBI qualifies him as a pirate, and I do love a pirate.*

On a whim, she walked up to Bud and leaned on the fence, close enough to him for a quiet conversation.

"Bud, it is curious how we keep running into each other."

"That's right," he said, looking up at her. He smiled briefly and then looked down at the ground again.

"The body in the landfill, the man wearing the Rolex watch. Who was it?"

"Alexa, we haven't released that information to the media yet. We're going to let them know as soon as my partner tells the Reverend."

"Can you tell me? Please?"

"Didn't come from me. Okay?" She nodded and Bud continued. "It was Jack Williams. You know, the mayor's environmental chief."

Alexa stared at the ground. She felt a sadness at not getting to know Jack Williams. The sadness left her quickly to be replaced by anger at the realization that Jack must have been murdered.

"You can't give me details, can you?" she asked.

"The only thing we're going to release is his identity."

"Understood," she said, "but I figure he was murdered."

"Alexa, that's all I can say. Can you tell me what you're doing here?"

"Chuck Porter got me involved," Alexa told him. "I should let him tell you exactly why I'm here."

"I'll ask him myself," Bud said and smiled as he motioned Chuck over.

"Hey, Bud," said Chuck, shaking hands with him.

"Alexa, why don't you go take that soil sample while I catch up with Bud here. We ain't seen each other since the party, an' there's been lots happening."

Alexa could hear them talking as she moved to DeMario's favorite swing and began filling a glass jar full of soil with a stainless steel spoon.

"Chuck, you heard 'bout Jack Williams, right?" said Bud.

"No, but I figured. What happened? Who could have done somethin' like that?"

"Well," said Bud, "we got some ideas. Anyway, Roscoe and I decided it would be better if he broke the news to Reverend Watkins personally—what with all Jack's done for this church."

Then Alexa heard a deep sob and looked up to see the Reverend leaning on the fence with his chest heaving.

Chapter 8

Alexa Grieves

Saturday, September 23

Mayor's aide found slain
by Gloria Conchita Ortiz

Two days ago, while investigating the presence of hazardous waste at the Cedartown landfill, the body of Johnson "Jack" Carter Williams was discovered. Williams' body had been buried there for at least two days but not longer than a week indicated Dr. Amos Caldwell, the Fulton County medical examiner who was called to the scene.

The body could not be brought to a hospital because of the possibility of its contamination by hazardous waste. Caldwell was able to perform an autopsy on site in a large tent reminiscent of the TV show *M.A.S.H.* His report suggested that Williams had met with foul play. Investigators from Cedartown, Polk County and the FBI continue to investigate.

Williams had served as the mayor's environmental boss and chief policy maker. He was directly responsible for (cont. on 3A, Aide)

Alexa read the short article twice but really knew no more than she had before. She sat at her desk feeling a bit numb, feeling something frightening and profound without knowing really what.

Alexa grieved for what she had missed with Jack. She didn't love him but would now never have the chance to know him better. Her throat thickened, and she started to cry. She pulled a tissue from a box in the drawer and dried her eyes. She stopped crying, but her heart still ached. She couldn't go on feeling pitiful; she had work to do. There were several reports that would be overdue unless she dug in really hard the next couple of days.

Alexa pulled up the newest report on soil contamination at Seitzman's Foundry in northwest Atlanta. The foundry had operated until the early 1980s, producing lead for manufacture into radiation shields for x-ray technicians and lab workers. An investigation of the soil near the foundry discovered lead at percent levels in the soil. The levels were much higher than she'd expected—as if they'd been throwing pure lead out the back door.

Alexa flipped to the front of the document and made a note of the address. She wanted to see the place. She checked her calendar and decided to drive out there when the phone rang.

CHAPTER 9

TRIP TO THE FOUNDRY

Monday, September 25

Bud knew the next step was to talk to Jimmy Ray and the best place to find him was the foundry that Melanie Groover had mentioned. *I'll bet Alexa Mason will know where it is*, he thought, but the thought of calling her made him a little nervous.

"AMM Environmental. Alexa Mason," she answered.

"Ms. Mason, it's Sergeant Bud Prior."

"Hello, Sergeant Prior. What can I do for you?"

"I'm looking for a foundry that's a hazardous waste site somewhere in Atlanta. Some environmental work's happening there, and they've got some new hires."

"That's easy. It's Seitzman's Foundry out near Bolton Road. Coincidence—I've got to go out there today."

"No other sites where they might be hiring?"

"Maybe a couple of others, but Seitzman's just got Superfund money and is looking to put on fifty workers. It's part of a big push to get it cleaned up before the election. You know, so the big-D Democrats can take credit."

"Ms. Mason, do you think I could follow you out there?"

"That would be fine, Sergeant."

Bud felt his heart beating hard in his chest at the thought of seeing her again. He was grinning and his face was flushed.

It took Bud a little longer to get to Alexa's office than he had planned. He found her leaning against her Toyota.

"Traffic," Bud told her as he rolled down his window.

"It's okay, Sergeant Prior," she said. She gave him a wave and got into her Corolla and turned the key. The starter motor turned over, but the engine wouldn't catch. She tried it several more times without success.

Bud watched her pound on the steering wheel in frustration. She got out and walked over to his government sedan.

"Toyotas are supposed to be reliable. Oh, well! How 'bout I catch a ride with you?"

"Sure." Bud smiled at her. "And I can give you a ride back here afterward. For this trip, why don't you call me Bud instead of Sergeant Prior? After all, you did give me a kiss on the cheek."

"I haven't forgotten that, Bud." She grinned. "I'll get my stuff."

Alexa got in the non-descript black g-car and put her sample case on the floor between her feet.

"So, where too?" said Bud.

"Head out I-75 to Moores Mill and take a left. We'll swing over to Bolton Road that way. The foundry's actually off South Atlanta Road."

"I can get us close," said Bud, "but then you'll have to direct me."

They drove in silence for a few minutes.

"Alexa, something came up the other day when we were out at that landfill. To work there, one would need HazMat training. What exactly is that?"

"You mean the forty-hour OSHA training?"

"I guess."

"Anyone who works in the field has to have the forty-hour course. They teach you a little chemistry, a little common sense, and give you the chance to put on some HazMat gear."

"Forty hours, hmm? So that's a whole week."

"Yes. It's boring to sit through, but you've got to have it. Required by law. You have to renew with an eight-hour refresher every year too."

"Thanks," said Bud and lapsed back in silence.

"So, Bud, when did you figure out you wanted to be a cop?"

"From the time I was a kid, I always wanted to be in law enforcement. My dad was a deputy in northwest Georgia. I went to college, and when I got out, I joined APD. I was working in Vice, Sex Crimes, and briefly in Homicide before I got transferred to Internal Affairs. I was in Internal

Affairs for the last seven years. I only started working with the feds about four months ago. For a single parent, the FBI's a little more family friendly than APD."

They rode along in silence for a few moments until Bud changed the subject.

"So tell me about the environmental business, Alexa."

"Well, Bud, my company has just two employees, Karyn and myself. Karyn's my administrative aide. She's a lot more than that. I couldn't do it without her."

"You must work pretty hard."

"I do, because it's my own business. I guess I don't even think about my hours. I just do what needs to be done. I work a lot—nights, weekends. AMM Services is pretty much my life. I've known for a while I'm ambitious."

"I figure you named the company with your initials. So what's the middle M stand for?"

"It's Margaret. My middle name." She laughed and blushed a little.

At a red light, they turned to look at each other. Their shared look was interrupted by the car behind them honking.

"Alexa, why don't you tell me your thumbnail history too?" Bud asked when they were on the interstate.

"Sure." She smiled at him again. "I went to college in Athens. I was a party girl all through college. I wasn't ready to leave Athens, so I got a master's in Environmental Health Science. I had one professor who was really inspiring. Dr. Smith. She didn't really push me in one direction or another, but she did make it clear that hard work would probably make more of a difference in consulting than any other kind of environmental job."

"How'd you start your business?"

"I worked for a big company out in Norcross for a while. It was pretty good work, and the company was doing well. They had some big contracts with the military. I dunno, Bud. What I was doing seemed like it was just generating paper without much basis in reality."

"Probably better money working for yourself, right?" said Bud.

"I'm actually not taking home as much money now. It's more rewarding in other ways. I can really make a difference. I feel like I really helped a child with lead poisoning. The hospital said he'd be okay. Helping that kid meant a lot more to me than any boring report I've ever written."

Bud was silent for a moment.

"Bud, I should tell you about this foundry," she said. "It used to produce lead aprons for x-ray workers, stuff like that. I also think they made fishing sinkers for a while. I've read a report on it, and the levels of lead in the soil out there are the highest I've ever heard of."

Bud took the curving exit ramp for Moores Mill Road. He was quiet until they got to the end of the ramp.

"Why is lead such a problem?"

"It's a huge problem for kids. Makes them violent and stupid. Some scientists think that some of the ADHD in kids is due to lead poisoning."

"That seems like a really simple answer," said Bud.

"True," Alexa told him. "I don't know the biology exactly, but kids who've been lead poisoned have IQ drops of up to ten points. It's a big societal problem as well. You've heard about all the lead paint in old buildings. Anyway, kids can get lead from paint, from soil, and from the water."

"So this kid you found, how did he get lead poisoned?"

"Kids ingest soil from hand to mouth activity after playing outside. A few kids have been known to eat a handful of dirt now and then on purpose. I think the dirt he contacted may have been in the church playground. That's what I was doing there, but, Bud, you have to keep it to yourself."

Bud pondered what she had told him. She might be young, but she had maturity, and like him, Alexa was passionate about her work.

A large brick building loomed off to the right.

"Turn in here," said Alexa.

A high chain link fence topped with razor wire surrounded the foundry property. A sign on the fence read "Weston—Protecting Your Health" in big letters. The site was on a small knoll overlooking the Chattahoochee River. An old stone building with half the roof gone stood in the approximate center of the fenced area. Near the building were several backhoes pulling up scoopfuls of the dirt and loading them onto large sheets of clear plastic. Workers in hazardous waste gear and respirators shoveled the dirt from the plastic sheets into metal drums. A forklift loaded the drums onto a waiting truck. In a corner of the lot stood a construction trailer and a hastily constructed outdoor shower for decontamination.

Bud pulled the car up to the trailer, got out, and went inside. Alexa trailed behind him.

"Sergeant Bud Prior, Atlanta Police Department," he told the man in the trailer, showing him his shield. "I'd like to speak to Jimmy Ray Groover. I think he works here."

"I'm Greg Parsons. I'm the project manager for Weston, the remediation company. I don't recall any Jimmy Ray," said the man, raising his lined, sun-reddened face from the sheaf of maps that covered the table.

"I think he just started working here," said Bud.

"Well, the excavation contractor just hired some people. I don't know them yet."

Bud raised his eyebrows quizzically.

Parsons consulted a clipboard.

"Here he is—Groover, J. R. Anyway, I'll let you ask your questions," said Parsons, "but I can't have any trouble here. I've got a schedule. Whatever you need to investigate, go for it and please finish quickly."

"I appreciate it," said Bud.

"Thing is, I can't let you go back there without hazardous waste gear. I don't think they give cops HazMat training. Who do you want to speak to first? Jimmy Ray or his boss?"

"I'll talk to Jimmy Ray first," said Bud.

"Have a seat and I'll have somebody fetch him."

Bud pulled out one of the folding chairs and watched while the man talked on a walkie-talkie.

"'Bout ten minutes," the man told him.

Bud watched Alexa speak briefly to the man, then don a blue HazMat suit, pick up her sample kit, and leave the trailer. She turned to him just before he left and winked at him through the facemask of her respirator.

Chapter 10

Jimmy Ray

Monday, September 25

Bud waited until a pudgy man with ruddy cheeks shuffled into the trailer.

"I'm Jimmy Ray Groover," said the man. "They said you wanted to see me."

"That's right. I'm Sergeant Bud Prior of the Atlanta Police, on detail to the FBI. Have a seat, Mr. Groover," said Bud, pointing to the stack of folding chairs.

"So, what's up, Sergeant?" said Jimmy Ray, pulling up a chair.

"We're investigating a murder. The body was found at the Cedartown landfill."

Groover narrowed his eyes. His pudgy face was filmed with fine red clay dust. Through the dust, his sunburned jowls and red nose bespoke many hours in the sun.

"Anyway," Bud continued, "I heard that you used to operate the bulldozer at the landfill. What do you know about the body that was found?"

"I heard about that," said Groover, "but I don't know nothin' 'bout it. Only thing in that landfill is household trash, far as I know. I still got no idea why they fuckin' closed it. Now I gotta drive all the way into Atlanta each day. It sucks, man."

"Mr. Groover, I'm not concerned about anything but the body. We think the Ku Klux Klan may have been involved in this killing. Do you know anything about that?"

"Now I heard some stories 'bout the Klan in Cedartown," drawled Groover. "Course I got no idea who's in it."

"You've never been in the Klan, have you, Mr. Groover?"

"No way! My wife wouldn't hear of it," the man answered quickly.

"How'd you get this job, Mr. Groover?"

"You know, friend of a friend. I heard they were lookin' for a good heavy equipment man here. I needed a job, so I jumped on it."

Bud consulted his notebook and found his notes from the landfill.

"Mr. Groover, I talked to your old boss, Gray Winters. He said you didn't have HazMat training. How'd you get a job at this place without it?"

"They gimme the training 'fore I started."

"But the training's a week long. You've only been working here, what, a week and a half?"

"I took it in three days. We sat and listened to that crap for twelve hours a day. Boring, man, 'cept for the videos of shit blowin' up."

"Mr. Groover, here's my card," Bud told him. "Will you call me if you think of anything else or hear anything else about the killing?"

"Sure, Sergeant."

Next, Bud asked Greg Parsons, the Weston manager, if he could talk to Jimmy Ray's boss.

"That'd be Claude Waters," said Parsons and sighed. "I'll have someone fetch him too."

Claude Waters operated the small excavation company that Weston had subcontracted for a portion of the digging. He was about six-two and whipcord thin with illegible tattoos on both arms. He walked into the trailer and stared at Bud. An unfiltered cigarette dangled from Waters's lower lip, and he squinted against the smoke. To Bud, he looked like a con.

"You already talked to Jimmy Ray Groover, right?" Waters said.

"That's right. And you're Claude Waters, right?"

"I am Claude Waters. I own the excavation bidnez."

"I'm Sergeant Bud Prior of the APD, on detail to the hate crimes unit of the FBI. You hired Jimmy Ray Groover, is that correct?"

"Yeah, that's right," said Claude. "I heard he was a good backhoe man."

"I'm looking into a murder. An Atlanta man was killed. Probably near Cedartown. I'm tryin' to find out about Jimmy Ray. He used to drive the 'dozer at the Cedartown landfill where the body was found."

"Okay," Claude said.

"How'd you meet Jimmy Ray?"

"In a bar. Place a lot of construction and demolition guys go. Good place to find some guys."

"What bar?"

"Uh, I can't remember the name. One of them titty bars on Fulton Industrial. You know, the one with the pink awning."

"You always do your hiring in strip clubs?"

"Yeah, I do, as a matter of fact. What do you think? I put an ad in the paper and weed through résumés . . . for guys to push a shovel? I can see right away if they got a strong back. I can talk to 'em for a minute or two and figure out what equipment they can drive."

"Mr. Waters, you always know so little about the guys who you hire?"

"Well, it's a job hunter's market, especially for heavy equipment men. There's more work than folks to do it. I can tell pretty quick if they know what they're doing. Besides, Jimmy Ray had a good reference from that guy in Cedartown."

Waters blew smoke out the corner of his mouth.

Bud could sense something fishy. It was obvious from Waters's hiring practices that if he wasn't a criminal himself, he likely employed criminals.

"Here's my card, Mr. Waters. You call me if you think of anything else."

Chapter 11

She Does Like Me

Monday afternoon, September 25

Bud stepped outside the trailer and looked around the foundry lot for Alexa. The HazMat gear she wore made her identical to all the other workers. Finally, he located her by her graceful movements in a back corner near the foundry building. She was scooping dirt into a glass jar.

Bud checked his watch. It was about fifteen minutes before he would have to leave to pick up Christopher from day care. He stared at the dirt beneath his feet and made some grooves in the loose soil with the side of his shoe.

Alexa waved and started toward him.

"I got the samples I need, Bud," she said when she came through decontamination. "I know you've got to pick up your son, so I planned to finish about now. Do you want to pick him up before dropping me? That would be fine."

"Let's see how the traffic is," Bud told her.

Both were silent until they were back on the interstate.

"Bud, I know you cops like Manuel's," she said. "If you didn't have somewhere else to be, I'd ask you to get a beer with me."

"I'd love to have a beer with you, but the after-school care charges a dollar a minute after five. Can I have a rain check?"

"Any time, Bud."

Roscoe was right—she does like me, thought Bud. They rode in silence back to her office, a comfortable silence it seemed to Bud. It also seemed to him that both of them were taking stock at that point, wondering whether to see each other again and where their growing friendship might lead.

There was little traffic, and they got back to Alexa's office quickly.

At the curb in front of her office, Alexa got out and walked around to Bud's side of the car. She put her hand on his.

"Bud, you still got my numbers?"

"I do," he said, thinking of the business card she had given him at Starbucks, which he had carried in his wallet ever since.

"Since you have somewhere to be at the end of the day, why don't you call me for lunch sometime?" Then she raised two fingers to her lips, kissed them, touched her fingers to Bud's cheek, and was gone.

Chapter 12

Alexa's Rising Star

Monday, October 9

In all, twenty-five children had been admitted to Grady Hospital with lead poisoning. The children were all African American. The group included one other boy from the Summerhill Primitive Missionary Baptist Tabernacle. *Why so many?* Alexa wondered as she read the story in the paper.

"Karyn, can you think of anyone who would poison these children deliberately?"

"I dunno, Alexa. A hate group maybe?"

"We don't know for certain that it's deliberate, but everyone knows the health risks of lead."

Karyn shrugged just as the phone rang.

"It's the CDC," she told Alexa.

"I'll take it in my office," answered Alexa.

"This is Alexa Mason," she said when she was seated.

"This is Dr. Bruce Forrest of the National Center for Environmental Health of the CDC. We got your name from the hospital referral report for the Tohler boy, the first one. Ms. Mason, you do know how many children are being affected, don't you?"

"Yes. Twenty-five so far. I was just reading it in the paper."

"Ms. Mason, CDC is worried this is just the tip of the iceberg. I know you've done some soil, water, and paint sampling. What did you find?"

"Dr. Forrest, I don't know the source of the lead with any certainty. I've been working on issues at a Superfund site with lead in northwest Atlanta.

I don't know if it's the source. I took a sample from it the other day, and as soon as I get the results back from the lab, I'll be able to compare it to the soil that I believe DeMario Tohler was exposed to."

"Would it help if you used the labs over here? There are enough children affected that CDC is treating this as an epidemic."

"Dr. Forrest, I got a sample with very high lead—percent levels—from a church playground that looked as if the dirt had been put there recently. I think it might be a good idea to check all the playgrounds these children used. Maybe the playgrounds are the source, but I just don't know yet."

"The lead in the fill dirt would have to be the same, chemically, as the lead from that Superfund site you mentioned to prove that's where it came from, right?"

"That's right. That would show a connection, but it doesn't show how the lead got from the site to the playground."

"Ms. Mason, I think the police need to know about this as well."

"There is someone you could call, Dr. Forrest. He's a sergeant with Atlanta PD, but he works with the FBI. His name is Bud Prior. I can give you his number if it would help."

"In the meantime, Ms. Mason, the CDC would like you to serve as a consultant. I'm empowered to offer you a contract of up to sixty days at your usual rates. I'd like to come to your office with my contracting officer and set this up."

Wow, thought Alexa, *I've made it to the big time. Maybe now I could afford to pay Karyn* and *save some money*.

"I'd be happy to help, Dr. Forrest. Thank you."

They set up an appointment for the afternoon, and Alexa gave him directions.

When she hung up the phone, she leaned back in her chair and mused about how the lead poisoning case of DeMario Tohler was helping her career.

The phone rang and jarred her out of her musings.

"Ms. Mason," came a female voice with a faint Latin accent, "I'm Gloria Conchita Ortiz. I work for the Atlanta newspapers. I've been readin' about these children bein' lead poisoned. They're all black. Think that means anything? I sure would like to talk to you about it."

"Give me your number," said Alexa, "and I'll call you back."

She hung up and called Chuck.

"Chuck, I've got a reporter wanting to talk to me about lead poisoning in black children. You know, like a hate crime. I haven't told her anything yet, but someone will talk to her. Better it was us. You want to come over here? Meet her together?"

"Yeah," he said distractedly. "Why is a reporter so interested?"

"I haven't talked to you about the Tohler boy because I'm waiting on some results from the lab, but I think the dirt in the playground may be the source of the lead."

"Holy shit!"

"Exactly. You know there've been twenty-five cases of lead poisoning among black children in the last couple of weeks?"

"Yeah, I know. I just didn't make the connection. Busy with other things."

"Chuck, I also got a call from the CDC this morning. They've hired me as a consultant."

"I'm on my way over, Alexa. Call the reporter and tell her to be there in an hour. That should give us enough time to figure out what to say."

Alexa changed into her interview clothes, a cream-colored silk blouse, black slacks, and heels that she kept at the office. She knew the clothes made her look good, and that gave her confidence. Chuck got there ten minutes later. Alexa offered him a cup of coffee.

"I can't say for sure, Chuck, but I think maybe this fill dirt comes from a foundry in northwest Atlanta. I'm reviewing a sampling report. There are percent levels of lead in the soil up there—about the same level as at the church playground. I took a sample from the foundry site three days ago. I won't know for sure until it comes back from the lab."

"So it's really not the church's fault?"

"Chuck, if whoever provided the fill dirt knew about the lead, then the church is just as much of a victim as the kids. How could the Reverend Watkins or his wife want to hurt these children? It's just not in their character."

"So what do we do?"

"We don't know who's guilty. The kids have to come first whatever we do." Her voice was firm.

"I understand, Alexa," he said.

"So how much should we tell the reporter? She'll be here soon."

"As little as possible," said Chuck.

An hour later, a slender woman with olive skin and dark eyes and a scruffy man with a big camera bag entered Alexa's office suite. Karyn showed them into the small conference room where Alexa sat with Chuck Porter.

"I'm Gloria Conchita Ortiz, from the AJC. This is Bill Jones. He'll be taking your picture, if that's all right," said the woman.

"Please have a seat, Ms. Ortiz," said Alexa. "Pictures would be fine. Would you like some coffee?"

"Please."

"This is Mr. Chuck Porter."

"Ms. Ortiz," said Chuck, standing up and reaching to shake her hand.

"What can I do for you?" said Alexa, once Karyn had brought in coffee.

Gloria began with some questions about Alexa's background—where she grew up, where she had gone to school.

"So these kids with the lead poisoning," said the reporter. "Where did the lead come from? Old paint in their houses?"

"It's hard to say, Ms. Ortiz. Lead paint is more of a problem in the northeast where there are a lot of older houses. The source of the lead is one of the things we're trying to figure out."

"Ms. Mason, we all know lead is bad for kids. Can you tell me why exactly?"

"The whole picture on the biology is still emerging, but lead affects brain development, IQ, and socialization. Children are exposed to lead from many sources—soil, water, air, and the food they eat. The real public health problem is for the kids who aren't too sharp already. The brighter kids could lose some IQ points, but the kids at the lower end can end up needing a lot of help and being a drag on society."

"Any of these kids like that?" asked Ortiz as the photographer stood and began discreetly shooting pictures of Alexa from several angles.

"I don't think so. I believe they're getting the medical care they need in time to prevent any permanent damage. But it really is a potential tragedy for all these families."

"Why all these kids at once? Why aren't there any white kids poisoned? Seems to me it might be deliberate. You think so, Ms. Mason?"

Alexa smiled at the reporter before answering. "That's really out of my area of expertise. We don't know the source of the lead or how the kids are coming in contact with it yet." Alexa caught Chuck's eye and noted his infinitesimal nod.

"But this could be a toxic assault. Isn't that right, Ms. Mason, if someone were doing this on purpose?"

"I think you need to ask that question to someone in law enforcement, not me." Alexa smiled at her again.

Gloria wrapped up the interview and thanked Alexa for her time.

"So, Alexa, do you think someone did this on purpose?" asked Chuck when the reporter had left.

"How would I know, Chuck? It would be an absolutely awful thing to do, right up there with murder."

"Twenty-five cases does seem like a lot, so I kinda get why the reporter asked that question. You were right to drop that hot potato."

He scratched his chin before continuing.

"Alexa, I don't know if the reporter came up with that on her own, but if the feds are investigating this as a hate crime, they need to know we gave that reporter nothing. That keeps our butts out of the sling."

He dialed and asked for Bud.

"Hey, Bud," he said after a short wait. "Chuck. I'm over here at Alexa Mason's office. We just met with a reporter about the lead poisoned kids. The reporter asked if the poisoning was on purpose. If people are thinking that way, maybe you guys need to be involved."

"Mm-hmm," said Chuck after a pause.

"Mick's at Underground. Right. Noon."

He hung up the phone.

"We're meeting Bud and Roscoe for lunch. We'll share information then."

"I can't stay too long, Chuck. I've got another meeting this afternoon."

Bud and Roscoe walked the three blocks from their office in the Richard B. Russell building to Underground Atlanta.

Old Alabama Street had been turned into Underground Atlanta, a pedestrian mall with bricks in lieu of asphalt. Mick's was a pricey restaurant with two floors of seating. On the patio at Mick's, one could look out over a rail at a large fountain and a plaza. The day was sunny and the weather just starting to turn cool. The plaza was crowded with people enjoying the first hint of autumn.

"So how much do you think Chuck and Alexa Mason know?" Bud asked Roscoe as they stood and waited.

"Probably about as much as we do, which isn't much."

"Roscoe, the guy I talked to at the foundry, Jimmy Ray, he somehow seems wrong. A little evidence and I'd peg him for the murder of Jack Williams."

"Jack Williams's murder isn't what they want to talk about," said Roscoe.

"Chuck said something about the lead poisoning in kids. You've seen it in the papers."

"Bud, how could that be a hate crime? So why do they want to talk to us?"

Bud shrugged in reply.

Alexa and Chuck were waiting outside. They shook hands all round and went into Mick's.

"Bud tells me you know something about lead poisoning," said Roscoe after they had ordered.

"Twenty-five kids, all black, have been admitted to area hospitals with high levels of lead in their blood," said Alexa. "You read about it in the paper. The Center for Disease Control asked me to be a consultant in this case because I brought the first kid to the hospital. You remember when I was taking samples at the church playground in Summerhill?"

Both Bud and Roscoe nodded.

"This is a huge number of lead poisoning cases for so short a time," she continued. "The reporter we talked to this morning asked me if it might be purposeful. The playground had fresh fill dirt, so I suppose it's a possibility.

"The Tohler boy likely contacted the lead in the fill dirt on the playground. Have these other kids been going to playgrounds? Maybe the playgrounds were worked on this summer and all these kids are suffering from the same fill dirt, if you know what I mean."

They were silent as the waiter brought their lunch and they all began eating.

"Alexa," said Bud after a minute, "do you have any idea who could be doing this? If—"

"Wait, Bud," she cut him off. "I didn't say that anyone was doing this. It was the reporter who authored that speculation."

"Okay, I understand that you want to be careful what you say, but if someone is supplying contaminated fill dirt to churches and schools, and I'm assuming these are black institutions because all the kids are black, then this certainly is something the hate crimes unit would be interested in. Where does the fill dirt come from?"

"I'm trying to figure that out." Alexa shrugged. "I've got samples of the soil from the foundry Superfund site at the lab and I'll compare those to the fill dirt from the Summerhill church playground. I may have to get some special analyses done, but that's no problem—the CDC has made their labs available."

"Ms. Mason," said Roscoe, "my understanding is that lead produces learning problems and antisocial behavior in children. Is that right?"

Alexa nodded.

"Look," Roscoe continued. "I'm not writing these kids off, but here's what I'm afraid will happen. The kids will never do well in school. They'll probably end up in a gang and be dead before they're twenty years old. If someone is doing this on purpose and knows what lead can do, then in a way, it's the same as genocide and it's definitely a hate crime.

"But," Roscoe continued, "there's no clear evidence that whoever's behind this knows what would happen to these kids the way you would, given your training. There's also nothing to suggest that anyone's behind this. It may all be a hideous, tragic mistake."

"You're exactly right, Agent Harriman. That's what I told the reporter."

"I was there," said Chuck in confirmation.

They ate in silence for a few moments.

"Alexa," said Chuck, "what sort of evidence would be needed to show these kids had been poisoned on purpose?"

"I told this to the CDC guy, Dr. Forrest, this morning. Someone has to check out where all twenty-five of these kids have been and what they did there. Then if the source of the lead was the same in all those places, I think the question for law enforcement would be how did the lead get there?"

The waiter came by to clear their plates, and Alexa excused herself.

"Give us a minute, Chuck?" asked Bud and began whispering to Roscoe. Chuck got up and went to the men's room.

"So how can this not be a hate crime, Roscoe?" asked Bud.

"If someone's doing it on purpose, it sure is. If someone's doing this knowingly, it's evil—and it's a hate crime.

"Again, we don't know yet, but if it is on purpose, it's worse than genocide. It's also about the guilt among those who are trying to help the children grow up right. Think how the Reverend Watkins and his wife feel about what happened to that boy."

"Roscoe, do we have any idea where to start?"

"Not really." Roscoe shrugged. "I think we're gonna be dependent on Alexa Mason for the science part of this. We need her knowledge and her experience. So it's a good thing she likes you." He reached over and squeezed Bud's shoulder.

"Cart before the horse," was Bud's reply.

Chuck and Alexa returned at the same time. They split the bill four ways and paid cash.

Outside Mick's on Old Alabama Street, Alexa addressed the three men.

"I don't know why," she said, "but I got a feeling someone's doing this on purpose. That reporter was right. Twenty-five kids is too many to be a coincidence."

PART II

Buffalo Soldier,
In a war for America
Buffalo Soldier,
Dreadlock Rasta,
Fighting on arrival,
Fighting for survival
—Bob Marley

CHAPTER 13

A PROPHET ARRIVES

Wednesday, October 11

Akbar Muhammad tossed his head, flinging his long dreadlocks over his shoulder. He drew a few stares from the people as he sauntered along Concourse D in Hartsfield-Jackson Airport away from the boarding tunnel.

Akbar had come to Atlanta because of the news accounts of the lead-poisoned children. Someone, he was sure, knew more about these poisonings than was being reported in the media.

Only black children had suffered, and inaction was not Akbar's way. Those responsible must bear the burden of guilt.

Akbar didn't have any luggage checked, just a single duffel slung over his shoulder. He walked to the MARTA station and took the train into town.

Akbar was the de facto head of a little known politico-religious group, the Jihad for Justice. He had converted to Islam at the age of twenty-three, two years after his mother had told him of his ancestry. Akbar was the illegitimate grandson of Minister Wallace Fard Muhammad, who, with his factotum, Elijah Poole, founded the Nation of Islam.

Akbar had circled the neighborhoods of all twenty-five lead-poisoned kids on a map of Atlanta. Churches would be the best places to start his quest; the ministers had the most influence with families. He made his way from the King Memorial MARTA station on foot toward the Summerhill Primitive Missionary Baptist Tabernacle.

Akbar knocked on the door of the tiny church. There was no answer, but he heard some movement inside. He was about to knock again when a large dark-skinned man, his jaw dotted with white stubble, opened the door.

"I'm looking for," he paused to consult his notebook, "the Reverend Rufus B. Watkins."

"I be Rufus Watkins," said the man, disapproval of Akbar's appearance evident in his tone.

"My name is Akbar Muhammad. I want to talk to you about the child from this neighborhood with lead poisoning."

"Mr. Chuck, he already been here 'bout that. Even brung the lady, Ms. Lexa."

"So, Reverend Watkins, you do know about the lead poisoning?"

"Yeah," said Watkins defensively.

"Maybe you could tell me about it."

"Mr. Muhammad, I don't know much. Not as much as Mr. Chuck."

"And Mr. Chuck is . . . ?"

"He be a friend who helps me. He a white man, an' he real smart. He's a detective."

"Reverend Watkins, could we go inside please? I just want to learn what happened." Akbar held his palms out to the Reverend.

"Wait jus' a minute. Why you be interested in what be goin' on in my church?"

"It's not so much your church as it is what has happened to the children. I'm concerned about the children. One of the boys in the neighborhood has lead poisoning. That may affect this boy's entire life. He's only one of many."

"I know. Ms. 'Lexa tol' me 'bout it. Also, I hear it on the news." Watkins's tone was belligerent.

Akbar realized the possibility that the older man felt challenged by the events.

"I been watching TV," the Reverend Watkins continued, "an' they don't make too a big thing of this."

Akbar stood, his hands open before him. He realized the Reverend Watkins was trying to decide whether to hear him out or not.

"Please," said Akbar.

"Okay, I'll tell you what I know," said the Reverend, his face softening. "C'mon in."

Akbar followed Reverend Watkins through the tiny sanctuary and into the room behind the altar. There was a long table and folding chairs.

"This is the fellowship hall. We can meet here. My wife, Hattie, usually makes lemonade in the afternoon. You like a glass?"

"I surely would, Reverend Watkins."

The Reverend left for a few moments and returned, followed by a woman of equal girth.

"This be my wife, Hattie."

"I am Akbar Muhammad. Pleased to meet you."

Hattie set a glass of lemonade in front of each man and left the room.

"Can I call you Akbar?" asked Watkins.

"Certainly."

"Well, you call me Rufus. Akbar, with a name like that, I cain't he'p but wonder if'n you ain't one o' them Muslims. You know, one o' Farrakhan's boys. But you don't look like it—no bow tie an' them dreadlocks."

"I am a Muslim," replied Akbar. "I believe in and practice Islam, but I am not associated with the Nation of Islam. My own religion is more private than that. The Nation of Islam believes that whites are devils. I believe we are all God's children, no matter what color our skin."

"So you got some religious angle on this, uh, the problem with the kids?"

"No angle, Reverend Watkins. But I am outraged that a great wrong has been brought upon these children."

"That lady, Lexa, she be real worried 'bout the boy. She say he got poisoned from the playground. I been real worried 'bout that too. I wouldn't do nothin' to hurt these kids. Playground's part of my wife's day care. 'Lexa said there was a problem wit' the dirt in the playground."

"Who is this lady?"

"A white lady Mr. Chuck bring round here. She knows 'bout kids gettin' sick 'n' all."

Akbar paused a moment.

"Reverend Watkins, the boy has likely been harmed. I know we both agree on that."

"Yeah, but it ain't none o' my doin'. I jus' got that fill dirt. I mean, the man be givin' it away, an' he deliver it too. We had to spend so much fixin' up the day care, well, that free fill dirt for the playground—it was a blessing."

"Free fill dirt, huh?"

"I been feelin' terrible 'bout DeMario Tohler."

"Tohler?"

"Yeah. You know, the boy in the hospital."

"Reverend Watkins, I think all the churches and all the parents and communities where this has happened will have to come together. More people need to know about what happened to these children."

"How you fixin' to do that?"

"We need to organize, march, demonstrate. It worked in the sixties with Dr. King. It'll work now. We need to let the news media know about the awful crime that has been committed against our children."

"Maybe you right, Mr. Akbar, but I don't know if that'll be enough. Will people pay attention?"

"We've got to make them pay attention. Reverend Watkins, all I need now is your support."

Akbar was aware of a quaver of excitement that had crept into his voice. "If it'll help these kids," said the Reverend, "then, yeah, I'll help you."

Akbar shook the Reverend Watkins's hand and silently gave thanks to God, whatever different faiths might choose to call Him.

Then, also silently, and in a place as deep inside himself as his faith in the deity, Akbar cheered in jubilant glee.

Chapter 14

Stakeout

Thursday, October 12

Alexa was at her desk, plowing through the thick report on Seitzman's Foundry. The report was as dry as red clay dust on an August afternoon. The engineer who had written the report had been unstinting in every detail in the descriptions of the site investigation. The foundry had been on the radar screens of both state and federal environmental regulators for six years. A number of investigations had been performed. The city was hoping that this one would be definitive and final.

The phone rang in the outer office. Alexa heard Karyn answer and then transfer the call. Alexa picked up the phone, happy for a distraction. It was George Torres, the foundry site manager.

"What can I do for you, Mr. Torres?" Alexa asked.

"I know the mayor's office has hired you to perform some limited oversight at the foundry."

"That's right."

"Do you think you could back us up on some confirmation sampling and keep it part of your contract?"

"You want me to sample after you?"

"That's right. Also, don't tell us what lab you're using. There's a big push here for an independent look. I guess they don't trust us."

"I'm happy to do it. You sure it's not a conflict of interest with me working for the mayor as well?"

"I checked it out, Ms. Mason. It'll be fine. The mayor's office knows and is expecting you to do it."

Alexa checked her calendar.

"I could do it late today, maybe this evening, but otherwise, it'll be a week before I can get to it."

"Late today would be preferable."

George gave her instructions on where he would put the key to the padlock on the front gate of the foundry site.

Alexa then called the mayor's office to double-check on the conflict of interest. They were expecting her call and told her that oversight at the foundry would be no problem. They also told her they would award her the extra hours to cover the work.

Reading the report took longer than Alexa expected. Finally, she closed the thick notebook and changed into jeans and boots. It was not until 7:30, getting dark, that she approached the foundry.

She opened the padlock on the gate with the key from a key box attached to the chain link fence, exactly where Torres had said it would be.

The sun was setting, and the thin cumulus clouds behind the skeletal remains of the foundry building took on vivid orange and then pale pink hues. A beautiful sunset over a hazardous waste site struck her as an odd combination. As she donned coveralls and a respirator, Alexa shuddered as she thought again of the twenty-five children whose lives and dreams and hopes had been shattered.

The sunset was fading, and she knew that darkness would come swiftly. Alexa consulted her sampling map and walked to the edge of the excavation. Samples needed to be taken from the walls of the excavation at various depths to ensure that the soil removal was going deep enough.

Alexa spooned soil into a clear plastic jar with a stainless steel spoon. She had just finished putting a chain-of-custody tag on the jar when she saw car lights on the road surrounding the foundry fence.

From her vantage point at the bottom of the excavation, she could clearly see what was happening, although she would be hidden from someone approaching the site.

A pickup truck drove along the back fence and then stopped next to a dump truck parked just outside the fence. Two men got out of the pickup and crawled under the fence through a small opening. One of them carried a flashlight and directed it at the backhoe. The other got on the backhoe and started it up.

She almost got out of the hole to ask them what they were doing, but an unwelcome sense of danger kept her still and silent.

The man on the backhoe filled the dump truck with dirt from the sheet of heavy plastic near the foundry building, lifting the bucket high over the chain link fence. That dirt had been dug out from very near the foundry building itself; it had the highest lead levels on the site. When the dump truck was loaded, the man parked the backhoe. Then the two crept back out under the fence. One of them got in the pickup and the other in the dump truck. The vehicles started and drove off.

Alexa stayed down in the pit until she saw the brake lights of the pickup come on at the site entrance. Her Toyota was parked behind some scrub pines at the other side of the gate.

She wondered why someone would be taking the soil at night. *Could these two be using this soil to poison the children?* she wondered.

The truck began to move.

I don't know what they're doing, but I can't let them get away, she thought.

Alexa sprang from the excavation, grabbing her sample kit but forgetting the one sample bottle she had only just sealed and tagged, and sprinted to her car. She dropped her boots, gloves, coveralls, and respirator at the gate and hopped in her Corolla.

Alexa caught up to the truck on South Atlanta Road and then stayed a hundred yards back as she followed them on a winding course through west Atlanta.

They parked the dump truck on a narrow dead-end street near the Clayton sewage treatment plant.

Alexa pulled over a hundred yards back and parked. She slouched down in her seat and watched as the man driving the dump truck got into the pickup. She crouched even lower as they drove past her.

When she watched them turn at the light, she followed. They drove straight out Bolton Road to Fulton Industrial. They headed south and parked at a Mama Gloria's, a nude dancing club just south of I-20. She watched the two men walk into the bar grinning.

Alexa hesitated for a moment and then remembered she had a hooded sweatshirt in the back of the car. It wasn't much of a disguise, but she put it on and pulled the hood over her head so that her face was mostly hidden.

She also pulled a twenty-dollar bill out of her purse and stuck it in the pocket of her jeans.

As she walked through the parking lot, she noticed most of the cars sported decals of the Stars'n'Bars, the confederate flag. The front of the bar was a mobile home attached to the front of a wood frame building. The building looked as if it had been added on to the mobile home. The outside walls were dingy. Above the front door was a large neon sign of the outline of a woman wearing a skimpy bikini that blinked on and off.

The place was smaller than she expected. It smelled of cigarettes and stale beer. At the end of the room was a small stage where a large-breasted blonde woman gyrated to "Stuck in the Middle with You" playing on an old Wurlitzer. The room was dark except for the stage lights. Blue wisps of cigarette smoke hung in the air.

"Five bucks cover," said the big man standing just inside the entrance

Alexa handed over the twenty and took her change, keeping her face down.

The two men she had followed were sitting next to the stage. She sat at a table where she could see both them and the door.

The chubby red-faced man got up and stuck a dollar bill in the blonde's garter. The stripper smiled down at him and licked her lips. The other man sported a long, greasy blond ponytail.

A waitress came by. Alexa kept her head down.

"Draft," she said in as deep a voice as possible.

When the waitress left, Alexa looked up. Another man had joined chubby and ponytail by the stage.

The man seemed familiar, but Alexa couldn't recall where she had seen him. The man was tall and thin. His head was shaved, and there were tattoos on his arms.

The thin man stood up and slipped a bill into the dancer's garter. She looked at his hand on her thigh and smiled. He beckoned, and she bent down as he whispered in her ear. The man sat down as the dancer continued jiggling in the spotlight.

When the song was over, the stripper walked off the stage and sat with the three men a moment. Then she took the chubby one's hand and led him through a doorway in the corner of the room next to the stage.

The thin man and the one with the ponytail began an animated conversation. Alexa was close enough to hear most of what they were saying.

"You can't figger out why I wanna do this," said the thin man with an edge in his voice. "Well, I'll tell ya. When I was eight, my daddy was taking my mother to the hospital. She was pregnant. Nigger driving a logging truck hit 'em full on. So me an' my sister, Joanne, had to go live with my Uncle John in Burnsville. I remember missin' my momma and daddy somethin' terrible.

"Fall of '79, I was fourteen. Uncle John got me up early, and we drove two hours to Greensboro. On the way, he told me the niggers and Jews were tryin' to take America away from us. Right in the middle of town, there were Klansmen all decked out in their white robes. Uncle John told me they was there to put a stop to the government handouts the niggers were getting. We parked the car, and Uncle John began introducing me to these Klan guys. He told 'em a nigger killed my parents and I was there to get payback.

"After a bit, a cop on a motorcycle came and told us that the cops were all going to lunch. We got in our car and drove along with other Klan guys down the street past the church where the niggers and the protestors was. We pulled over, an' my uncle gave me a shotgun and told me what I had to do. I been findin' ways to take care of the nigger problem ever since."

The man's story made Alexa feel nauseous. She vaguely remembered hearing about a massacre in Greensboro. She also knew the real question was whether this man's story could link him to the poisoned children.

Alexa got up and chose a path to the door that would take her close to the stage to get a better look at the thin man. She had to squeeze in between two chairs to get by the small round table where the men sat. As she passed, the man turned around, feeling pressure on the back of his chair.

He looked up right into Alexa's face, smiled, and grabbed her wrist.

"Hey, sweetie," he said, "why don't you sit down and have a drink with us?"

"I've got to be somewhere," said Alexa. She twisted her hand, trying to pull away from the man, but he only held her tighter.

"Just a quick drink," he said.

"No," answered Alexa.

"Look, we're not gonna hurt you," said Ponytail. "We just want some company."

"One drink only," said Alexa and sat down. "Just a Coke," she told the waitress who appeared a second later.

"Awwww," said Ponytail, leering at her.

"You guys got names?" asked Alexa when the music stopped.

"I'm Claude," said the thin man who had grabbed her arm. "This here is Face." Claude pointed to Ponytail.

"I'm, uh . . . Margaret. So what do you guys do for a living?" she asked.

"Construction," said Claude. "Backhoe work. Whadda you do?" he asked. "Ain't too many women cute as you come here."

Alexa stared at the thin man and realized why he seemed familiar. He had been the backhoe operator that day at the Cedartown landfill. She studied him as he drank his beer.

"This and that," she told him. "I get by."

"That's what I do too," chimed in Face. "Whatever I can to get a little money. Claude here been keepin' me busy lately."

Alexa noted the sharp look Claude gave Face.

"So . . . uh, Margaret, whadda you say we move this party?" asked Claude. "I got a motel room just down the street. Ya wanna get freaky?" He reached over and began stroking her wrist with his index finger. "I'll bet you can go all night, and there's two of us," he pointed at Face, "to pull this train."

Alexa said nothing and kept her eyes low. She wasn't sure how to get out of there. Claude wasn't big, but he looked strong. She reached surreptitiously into her purse and set off her beeper.

"Oops. Gotta go." She jumped up from the table, bumping it with her knees and dumping almost all of her Coke in Claude's lap.

She was out the door of the bar and running for her car before anyone could react.

She started her car and parked in a gas station across the street where she could still see their pickup truck.

Alexa dozed as she waited. It had been a long and full day, and with the inactivity, her fatigue caught up with her.

She awoke with a start. The pickup truck was gone.

Alexa drove back to the Clayton plant and found that the dump truck was also gone. The only sign it had been there was the presence of a few small piles of reddish soil on the street. She took a baggie from her sample case and gathered some of the loose red dirt that peppered the asphalt where the dump truck had been parked.

Alexa turned the key in her Toyota to head home, planning to call Bud Prior in the morning. The car was dead. Just like the other day when Bud had given her a ride to the foundry.

"Shit! Shit! Shit!" She pounded on the steering wheel in fury.

When she reached in her bag for her cell phone, she realized she had left it back at the office. She tried to think and realized it would be only her word that the dump truck had ever been there. She pulled an envelope from the glove compartment, sealed the baggie inside it, and put the envelope in her purse. She thought about walking on Bolton Road to that strip mall on Marietta Street. It wasn't that far, only about a mile.

Alexa took her purse and sample kit with her. She had taken only a couple of steps toward Bolton Road when she saw a tall black man with dreadlocks striding along. He turned and looked at her, and in the thin glow of the streetlight, she saw him frown.

The man turned and came toward her. She thought about going back to her car, getting in and locking the doors, but the man conveyed no threat, no predatory aura of hostility, unlike Claude and Face. This man smiled as he approached.

"Miss! Miss!" he called out. "I don't think this is a good place for you after dark."

He had a slight Jamaican accent, and his broad handsome face beneath his dreadlocks showed humor and concern for her.

"No choice," she told him. "My car broke down."

"I could look at your car. Maybe it's somethin' easy I could fix."

"I would be grateful," said Alexa.

He lifted the hood and stared at the engine. The hood shadowed the engine, and Alexa could not understand how he could see anything.

He reached into the engine. She could see he was concentrating because the small pink tip of his tongue protruded from the side of his mouth.

"Try it now," he said after a few moments, pulling his hand out of the engine and wiping it on the leg of his jeans.

She got in, and the car fired right up.

"What'd you do?" Alexa asked him.

"You had a loose wire on the coil. I used to have a car like this, back in Chicago."

"I'm really grateful," she said.

"Well, it's late," he said, "and you don't seem like the type of woman who would walk around here at night."

She drove off, leaving her dread-locked savior on the sidewalk.

Friday, October 13

The phone rang just as Bud got to his desk the next morning.

"Prior, FBI."

"Bud, this is Alexa. I've got to tell you what I saw last night."

"What's on your mind, Alexa?"

"I think I saw the people who take the fill dirt to the churches. You know, the ones who are possibly poisoning the kids."

"Tell me about it."

Alexa spent a half hour relating what she had seen.

"I couldn't stay with them because I fell asleep."

"Alexa, you shouldn't have done that. It was dangerous, and it could be considered interfering with an investigation."

"Maybe you're right, Bud. But if they are the poisoners, now I can identify them. Can you look for the dump truck? I can get the soil analyzed."

"You don't have a plate number, huh?"

"Oh, no," she groaned. "I was thinking about following the men. It was dark. I didn't . . . didn't get the license plate."

"Alexa, what did you prove by seeing them at the bar? It's a known hangout for hookers. That's why they came on to you. We can't do much with your story. I do believe you, but that doesn't really matter."

"Bud, please. The dump truck has another load of poison. Think of the kids."

"There's no proof at all that the soil in the truck has anything to do with the children. Sorry, Alexa, but there's nothing I can do."

As soon as Alexa hung up after talking to Bud, her phone rang.

"Alexa, this is George Torres. I found a sample jar with your tag on it. It was left in the excavation pit, and your boots 'n' stuff were by the gate. Not cool."

"Oh, hell! I'm sorry, George. Look, I've got to check on an analysis the lab's doing for me. Why don't I stop and pick up the sample jar and my stuff on the way?"

Alexa debated telling Torres about the lead-poisoned kids and the possible connection to the foundry.

At the foundry, she was talking to George Torres near the decon area when she felt a pair of eyes on her. She turned to find a man staring at her. It was Claude from the bar. In the daylight, she could see blue veins snaking along his thin muscular arms. He wore black jeans and engineer boots. His shirt was off. As well as the myriad tattoos on his arms, a small iron cross was tattooed high on his back near his left shoulder blade. The man continued to stare at her as he donned HazMat gear.

When the man got the Tyvek suit over his shoulders, he grinned at her and cupped his genitals before donning his gloves and respirator. She shook her head and realized Bud was right. She shouldn't have followed the dump truck.

"Alexa," said George Torres. "I've had your boots and gloves deconned, but I'm afraid your respirator got some dirt in it."

"I'm really sorry, George," she said. "I got distracted last night. I had to leave the site quickly. I was planning to come back, but I had car trouble."

"There's no problem with the sampling you did, is there, Alexa?" His tone was full of concern.

"None. I had just finished taking this last sample. You see the bottle is tagged and sealed. The others are in my kit back at the office and I'll get them to the lab today."

She read worry in his face.

"Don't worry, George. There's no problem." She touched his shoulder reassuringly.

"Thanks, Alexa."

She loaded the sample into a cooler of dry ice in her car and drove to the CDC lab that was doing the comparison analysis between the foundry soil and the sample she had taken under the swing in the playground at the Summerhill Primitive Missionary Baptist Tabernacle.

This lab was able to do the complex speciation analysis of the lead in the soil. It was an expensive analysis, but the CDC was footing the bill.

Alexa parked at the lab.

"We've been expecting you, Ms. Mason," said the receptionist. "Your analysis is done. Doctor Smith wanted to talk to you about it."

"These samples are real curious," the chemist told her when she was seated in his office. "The difference is the total lead concentration in the second sample, AM001-B2, is about 75 percent of that in the first sample. The second sample also has high levels of iron and cadmium. The real curious thing is that the ratios of the anions are identical between the two samples. That's the real giveaway that they came from the same source. We did a lead speciation, and there's a 95 percent similarity between the two. What I figure is that the second sample is the same as the first one with some other dirt added."

Alexa flipped through the lab report. The first sample was from the foundry, and the second sample from the playground.

"So, Doctor Smith, you could conclude that the second sample was identical to the first, just a little diluted, perhaps by mixing with some other material that contained the other metals."

"That's exactly what I'd conclude, Alexa."

"Thanks, Doctor Smith. This is really helpful."

"This got something to do with those kids?"

"I can't say just yet."

She drove back to her office and wrote the report on the two samples. It only took an hour. When she was finished, she called Chuck, told him about it, and sent the report over to him by courier.

She also called Bud back. It was early afternoon, and he wasn't there. She left a message that chemical analysis by the CDC supported the foundry soil being the likely source of the lead in the playground.

CHAPTER 15

A SERIOUS MEETING

Monday, October 16

It was not yet nine in the morning when the phone in Alexa's office rang. Karyn was not yet in, so Alexa picked it up.

"Ms. Lexa," said the Reverend Watkins, "there's gonna be a meetin' this Wednesday night."

"What kind of a meeting?"

"We need to get people knowin' 'bout what happened to the children."

"So something can be done?"

"Yeah, we want some action!"

"Reverend Watkins, I'll be happy to come to the meeting. I'm curious though. Earlier, you didn't want any publicity. Why did you change your mind?"

"This fella Akbar. He came by the church. He convinced me. You'll meet him."

"Reverend Watkins, I'd be pleased to be at the meeting."

"One other thing, Ms. Lexa. There'll be lots of folks there. Could you maybe talk about . . . you know?"

"The lead in the playgrounds, Reverend?"

"Yup. You know more 'bout it than anybody."

The meeting was to be held at a Baptist Church near Greenbriar Mall. Watkins gave her directions.

Just after she hung up with the Reverend Watkins, the phone rang again. It was Mrs. Tohler.

"You know 'bout the meetin'?"

"I just heard about it from the Reverend Watkins. I'm planning on being there."

She called Chuck afterward to confirm the directions, and he told her the FBI would also be there.

Chapter 16

A Prophet Speaks

Wednesday evening, October 18

Alexa arrived at the meeting. The pastor of the Greenbriar Baptist Church, Josiah Smith, and Reverend Watkins met her outside. They walked into the large basement that served as the meeting room. She surveyed the room with chairs set in rows with a center aisle. There was a table up front and a podium with a microphone.

"Come meet Akbar," said Reverend Watkins. They walked to the front of the meeting room where, in the front row, sat the tall man with dreadlocks who had so handily and quickly repaired Alexa's Toyota several days ago.

"Reverend Watkins," said the man, standing and shaking the minister's hand.

"Please meet Ms. Alexa Mason," said Watkins. He gestured at the dark-haired woman. "This is Mr. Akbar Muhammad."

"Again, a pleasure, Ms. Mason," said Akbar.

"We met already," said Alexa and laughed. "You fixed my car."

"I was happy to do so," Akbar told her. "Why are you here, Ms. Mason?"

"I'm an environmental consultant. I'm investigating the lead poisoning. Now, Mr. Muhammad, I'll ask you the same question."

"Well, I'm doing the same as you. Protecting the children. It was a coincidence, our meeting like that." He smiled.

"Boy, I'll say." Alexa smiled back.

By the time the meeting was supposed to start, the room had filled to capacity. People were still coming in, standing in the aisles.

"I need to start this meetin' and introduce you to all these folks," said the Reverend Watkins to Alexa. "I told you I want you to say something here. You be the one who really listened to Ms. Tohler. I didn' tell you before, but they've been several folks went with Mistah Chuck over to Ms. Tohler's, and they couldn't find nothin' wrong with DeMario.

"I'm glad you know Akbar already, but I be worried he turn white folks off. We got to do something about the children, but I didn't know exactly what till Akbar came."

"Reverend Watkins." Alexa looked up at and smiled. "I do want to help you, but I think we need to know what the plan is. I want you to know I'm with you 100 percent. I'll also be honest with you. If I think Akbar's plan is good, I'll support it. If not, I'll tell you what I think is wrong with it. The most important thing is to make sure that the people who have the power to help the children get the right message. That's what I want to help you do."

"It sure would be important, you being the one who figured out what was wrong. We wouldn't be doing this without you."

"Reverend Watkins, it would be wrong for me to do anything else. There's another thing too—you and I have to talk about the fill dirt, where it came from."

"I know, Ms. Lexa. Later." A shadow of guilt crossed his face. "I'm gonna talk first, Ms. Lexa, and I'll introduce you when I finish."

Alexa sat in the back row on the left. When the Reverend Watkins finished speaking, he motioned for her to come up front.

"I want to thank Reverend Watkins for letting me speak to you tonight. I'm not part of the government, and I'm not with any church. I'm a scientist, and Reverend Watkins asked for my help. I think I understand what may have happened.

"What I'll give you tonight are facts, only facts. What I know is based on evidence I've discovered."

A large woman in the second row raised her hand.

"Tell us what we should do for our kids."

"Take them to Grady Hospital," replied Alexa. "Grady is now set up to do blood lead screening at no charge. If there's a problem, Grady is the best place to have your children treated. The doctors at Grady are all aware of this. I know many of you are already going to Grady for treatment. You should do whatever the doctors say.

"But I'm not a doctor," she continued. "What I'm trying to do is figure out how your children were poisoned in the first place in order to make sure no other children are harmed. I have evidence for three children, the ones at Reverend Watkins's church. Reverend Watkins asked me to test the soil in the church playground. It is possible that the soil is the reason the children are sick."

She paused and looked around the room. It was quiet enough to hear a pin drop. She saw Akbar Muhammad cover his eyes with one hand as if weeping.

"Reverend Watkins told me he got some fill dirt to build up the playground, but the dirt in the playground is one possibility. I don't know for sure yet. What I will tell you is that I will not stop until I've figured this out and we can keep more children from being harmed."

She paused a moment for more questions, but there were none.

"If any of you know anything about whether your churches received any fill dirt or where the dirt came from, please let me know. I'll be around after the meeting or you can contact me through Reverend Watkins."

The audience was quiet and respectful, heads nodding in assent as she finished.

Alexa sat down. She'd done what she'd been asked to do and hadn't gone out on a limb. She was pleased with what she had said.

Reverend Watkins got up from his seat in the front row and introduced Akbar.

Akbar walked slowly up to the podium. His steps were stately and measured. He reminded Alexa of an African king.

Akbar wore a dark gray suit and a thin knitted tie. His dreadlocks were tied back, and the heavy ponytail bounced slightly with the rhythm of his walk. Standing at the podium, he surveyed the audience.

"You know why we are gathered here today," Akbar began in his lilting Jamaican accent. He paused and surveyed the audience again. He smiled and his teeth gleamed whitely against the dark bronze of his skin.

At that moment, Alexa again became conscious of his personal power and attraction.

"It is the greatest sadness that brings us together. God tells us that some good must come from everything, but right now, I cannot see how the evil that has been done to our children can yield anything of good."

Alexa turned in her chair and saw Bud Prior. He was seated in the back row, but on the other side. Their eyes met, and he nodded to her.

"It is not enough to be aware of the problem," Akbar continued. "It is not enough to obtain medical care for our affected children. It is not even enough to bring the perpetrators of this hideous crime to justice.

"What will be enough is when the toxic legacy of our industrial age is no longer borne unfairly by people of color. During Jim Crow, society shoved the black man to the back of the bus. Now, environmental racism is just another way to tyrannize people of color. This assault on our children, my friends and fellow sufferers, is where we must draw a line in the sand."

There was scattered applause and a collective "Amen." Akbar smiled at the audience again before he continued.

"What must we do now?" His voice was lower, and the audience strained forward as one to hear him. "My friends, we can do nothing yet ourselves, however much we would like to take action. But we must let those in authority know what has happened. We must realize that this evil is the work of a few who have strayed from the path of goodness, of love for one's fellow man. We ourselves will not stray from that path; it is only a misguided few who have done this evil deed. We will take the high road, casting blame only when we are certain that we know who committed this evil."

The audience was silent as Akbar paused again. Alexa marveled at how he could control the emotions of his listeners.

"We must tell those in control, those in law enforcement, those in government and those in the public, the good people who know right from wrong. I have misgivings—and I know you probably do as well—about involving the institutions of our government, the institutions of the white man. But this battle is one we must fight and win in the hearts and minds of the public. It is only by having the people of this nation, both black and white, on our side that we will prevail.

"Of course, my friends and fellow sufferers, we cannot forget the children whose lives have been permanently damaged. Their heartbreak will never go away.

"In the beginning, I told you I could not conceive of any possible good that could come out of this. Now I realize that these poor children will be the champions of our plight. That is the good that will come out of this. With the sad faces of these poisoned children, we will win the hearts and minds of the American people.

"The good that may come out of this is justice for our people, justice that has escaped us for so long. Well, now we are due."

The hall broke into spontaneous cheers.

"And how are we to let the American people know," continued Akbar after the applause had died down. "How shall we, in the midst of our grief for the loss of our children's potential, enable justice? For it is justice we want. Not merely the word justice, but the acts and deeds of men that shall redress the grievance our children must live with for the rest of their lives. Not merely justice for the children, justice for all people of color in our struggle against the terrible blight of environmental racism, against the toxic assault on our race, against the injustice that we live with daily and throughout our lives. That is the justice we seek, and only that will be sufficient."

He paused again. The audience was rapt and silent.

"We shall seek justice without anger or violence. We shall seek justice with the sincere hope that mankind will never again witness such an evil. My friends, our numbers are not large, yet we can speak with the mighty voice of a multitude. A week from this Saturday, on October 28, we will march from the Summerhill Primitive Missionary Baptist Tabernacle, where this tragedy began, to the state capitol. We will let everyone know what we are doing. With your permission, my friends, I will obtain a permit from the city for this march. Everything will be done in a forthright and honest way. The press, the government, and the public will see this evil for what it is. The outcry will be too great for the American people and for any politician to ignore. That is how we will succeed, my friends.

"Reverend Josiah Smith of the Maranatha Primitive Baptist Church will give you the details of the march. I want all of you there. We have a responsibility to our children, both those who have been affected and the ones we now seek to protect, to share our knowledge of this injustice with the world.

"Together we can triumph and seek the proper resolution to our sorrow. Together, we can find justice. Together, my friends, together."

Alexa looked around at the spellbound audience. There was not a dry eye in the room, and several of the women were openly weeping.

A few people began to clap when Akbar had finished but stopped when the rest of the audience refrained. It seemed inappropriate somehow, like clapping after a church service. Alexa could sense both the embarrassment and the raw emotion they held within. Akbar had combined the rah-rah enthusiasm of an athletic fan with moral outrage and a sense of righteousness.

Emotionally wired, most people sat quietly for a few minutes, then got up and milled around the hall, unable to let go of the feelings Akbar had stirred in them.

Alexa walked over to Bud. He was talking to the black FBI agent she had met at Mick's.

"Did you find out anything about the dump truck?" she asked him.

"We did drive over to where you said the dump truck was parked by the sewage treatment plant," Bud told her.

"Well, I told you it was gone," said Alexa.

"Miss Mason," said Roscoe, "could you identify the men?"

"Of course."

"We can use that eventually, but until we get some suspects, I don't know what to do with it."

"I don't know either," said Bud.

"The skinny guy had an iron cross tattoo," said Alexa. "You've seen him. He drove the backhoe at the Cedartown landfill when . . . you know. He also works at the foundry."

"I think I do know the guy," said Bud. "Seemed like a skinhead."

"That's him," chimed in Alexa.

"I'm sorry," Roscoe told her. "There's really nothing we can do."

Alexa clenched her fists. With the dump truck gone, she had lost her credibility with the feds.

"It was dark. I wasn't expecting to see anyone out there. I figure I did pretty well just to follow them."

"I'm sorry too, Alexa," said Bud.

The three of them were standing there when Akbar walked up.

"You gave me a terrific lead-in," he told Alexa, smiling broadly. Again, she was struck by Akbar's handsomeness up close.

"I didn't know how much to tell them. I figured it'd be best just to lay out the basic facts. I wanted to keep it simple."

"It was great," Akbar told her. "Perfect."

Alexa glowed with his praise.

The Reverend Watkins was standing next to Akbar.

"Akbar, Agent Roscoe Harriman and Agent Bud Prior of the FBI. They're looking into this."

"Gentlemen, I am Akbar Muhammad," he said, beaming and shaking their hands.

"That was quite a speech, Mr. Muhammad," said Roscoe.

"Thank you."

"Reverend Watkins, do you mind if you and I and Mr. Muhammad talk outside for a minute?"

"No, Agent Harriman. Is anything wrong?" asked Akbar.

"Not really. I just need a moment of your time, Mr. Muhammad."

Roscoe steered Akbar outside, leaving Bud and Alexa standing there. She stared at Bud for a moment.

"Bud, I've got some soil from where the dump truck was parked. Should I have it analyzed?"

"When did you take the sample? After the truck was already gone. There's no way to tie it back to the truck."

"I was afraid you'd say that," she said glumly. "The soil at the church is pretty similar chemically to the foundry soil."

"Still, Alexa, we have to show it came from the foundry and was given to the church with malice aforethought."

She nodded and lightly touched the back of his hand before walking away.

Agent Harriman, the Reverend Watkins, and Akbar Muhammad stood just outside the church, a little off to one side.

"So what's this all about?" asked Akbar.

"This march you're planning," Roscoe answered him. "Is it such a good idea? Look at what happened at all the other marches. Remember when Hosea Williams led that march in Forsyth County? Of course you'll publicize it, and it'll bring out all sorts of crazies—"

"Wait a minute," broke in Akbar. "We're just exercising our right of free speech."

"Agent Harriman and the FBI been looking into this from the git-go," said Reverend Watkins. "He's also been checking out what happened to Jack Williams."

"Who's Jack Williams?" asked Akbar and then cut off his own question. "Never mind. It really doesn't matter."

"It do matter," said the Reverend Watkins hotly. "If Jack Williams was still around, he'd know what we ought to do. Due respect, Mr. Muhammad, but the only reason we're listening to you is because Jack Williams is dead."

Akbar stared at him a minute. Jack Williams was clearly somebody important to the church.

Akbar turned to the FBI agent and softened his voice.

"Agent Harriman, what choice do I have about the march? I've got to follow through. I'm thinking about these children. How else will the situation change?"

"Well, Mr. Muhammad, the Bureau is not without resources, and we've taken an interest in this as a hate crime. The reason I don't want you to do the march is that it'll bring all sorts of crazies out of the woodwork. A bunch of redneck wannabes will confess to this crime once it's made so visible. The Bureau's job will be a lot harder. Don't you want the ones who did this brought to justice?"

Akbar looked at Roscoe for a long moment before he spoke.

"Agent Harriman, there's more to it. Can't you see that these kids are a symbol of what is being done to people of color in this country? Our race is forced to live with a poor quality environment . . . toxic waste, polluting industry close by, ugliness. It's another insidious form of racism, and most people don't know it's even happening."

"Look," said Roscoe, exasperated, "it's clear you don't really want to help these kids, their families—"

"Wait a minute!" the Reverend Watkins cut in. "Roscoe, don't you be talking out of line here. In spite of what I said about Jack Williams, Mr. Muhammad convinced me he cares. These kids, well, they're a symbol for racism, like he says. That's all."

Roscoe's lips compressed to a thin tight line, and he stared at Akbar.

"I know you have another agenda," said Roscoe, leaning close to Akbar and whispering. "I know it won't deter you to know the FBI is treating this as a hate crime. We can't fix everything that's wrong with America for the black man by using these kids. What we can do is find out who did this terrible thing, and holding this march sure won't help us in that effort."

Chapter 17

A Prophet Dreams

Wednesday night, October 18

Alexa waited outside the church. Although Akbar's words were stirring, she did not entirely trust his motives. He walked out and joined her in the cool evening air.

"Mr. Muhammad, I wanted to thank you again for your help. My car starts up every time since you fixed it. Thanks."

"It is curious we first met like that."

"True, but now I was wondering about a couple of other things. First, you don't look like a Muslim."

"Please call me Akbar, Miss Mason. I am the leader of the Jihad for Justice. We have a different agenda than the Nation of Islam, less radical, more in touch with the earth. The Nation of Islam members are guarded about their spiritual side and have no tolerance for strangers. Unlike them, the Jihad for Justice believes in tolerance for everyone."

"Seems like a pretty poor choice of names. 'Jihad' doesn't really seem like it means tolerance."

He was silent and Alexa continued.

"So it's really the well-being of these children that brought you to Atlanta?"

"I feel a great wrong is being visited on the children of my race. I seek to right that wrong."

Her eyes narrowed in skepticism.

"So where does the Jihad for Justice get funding?"

"Miss Mason, you do cut to the chase." He laughed, a rich throaty sound. "Honestly, I don't worry about it. Allah provides me the resources to do what he feels I must do. I don't question his ways; I just have faith. I act in ways I believe to be true to his purpose. To answer you specifically, the Jihad for Justice survives on donations. That's why I fly standby and don't have a rental car."

"You still haven't told me what you're doing in Atlanta. Not specifically."

"As you have not told me, Miss Alexa Mason, what you were doing out on Bolton Road after dark."

"Touché."

Reverend Watkins and Mrs. Tohler came out of the church and joined them.

"How's DeMario doing?" Alexa asked her.

"He's been home from the hospital for two days now. He seems much better."

"I'm glad to hear it. DeMario's a sweet kid."

"I'm sorry about what he did to you, and I'm grateful for all you done, Ms. Lexa."

Mrs. Tohler beamed at Akbar. "Your speech was wonderful, Mr. Muhammad. It made me think of Martin."

Alexa realized that Mrs. Tohler must have been deeply moved. Martin Luther King Junior was an icon for all African Americans. Comparing anyone to Martin was almost sacrilege. But Mrs. Tohler and her son had been deeply affected by the tragedy, and Akbar had seemed to speak directly to her.

"Thank you, Mrs. Tohler. I appreciate your kind words, but I doubt if I could ever measure up. I just hope God did speak through me tonight. I know what we have to do, and I just had to let you good people know what God put in my heart. Your boy was one of those affected, and I'm sorry."

"Thank you, Mr. Muhammad, but he's getting better now. Ms. Lexa, she helped out a whole lot."

The church was emptying out. People passed them, stopping to congratulate Akbar and shake his hand.

"It was an incredible speech, Akbar," Alexa told him.

"It's not entirely me. When I'm engaged in the right cause, God speaks through me. Like I told Ms. Tohler."

A Toxic Assault

Alexa sniffed. She wasn't religious. When she had been a little girl, Lois Mason, her mother, had always checked that Alexa said her prayers. Until eight years old, Alexa had been scrupulous about nighttime supplications, but at the age of nine, she discovered that she could neither confirm nor deny the existence of a deity. So Alexa stopped praying at ten and found it made absolutely no difference in her life.

Alexa's parents were Jewish, but they practiced their religion sporadically and at those times when Lois Mason felt guilty about neglecting the faith she had been born into but with which she felt almost no spiritual connection. Little wonder that Alexa grew up conflicted about religion.

From her father, Jack Mason, she learned kindness and humanism. He worked as a freelance technical writer and made a pretty good living at it, albeit with long hours. The time he spent with his daughter was precious. From him, Alexa also learned two things—to write the English language with grace and precision and to view ambition as a virtue. She continued to be grateful to her dad for the effortless way she was able to communicate her thoughts.

"Akbar," she said, "you realize this is still about these kids. They're the most important ones here. All this talk about justice is fine, but a crime was committed against these kids. In your speech, you made it clear that you have another agenda."

"The children are not my only agenda. You are perfectly correct. The children shall be the heralds of—"

"See that's what I'm worried about. I don't want these kids or their families to be used. I'm not a major player here. I know as this thing moves on, I'll be used by you, by the FBI, probably by the media too. Fine, but I don't want these kids to be used."

"May I call you Alexa?"

She nodded yes.

"Alexa, my ideas are not that radical. Can you deny that what is needed is a new kind of thinking in this country? We keep up the belief that our industrialization is a wonderful thing. It is not; it is a bad thing. It is evil.

"Have you ever read a poem by Robert Lowell called, 'For the Union Dead'? It is a comment on technology and its unintended consequences and how man cannot control it. The last line reads: 'A savage servility slides by on grease.' The earth cannot sustain the technology and the waste it creates. The disadvantaged have to deal with this waste most directly.

"Your car, the one I fixed. Eventually, it will be reprocessed and the waste will be stored in Tifton, Georgia, right next to a black community. Since you're from Georgia, how about Woolfolk Chemical?"

"I wrote the first Woolfolk risk assessment, Akbar."

Alexa recalled that early in the twentieth century, the Woolfolk chemical company in Fort Valley, Georgia, produced arsenic-based pesticides for agricultural use. The finished arsenic products were carried on an open-air conveyor belt to the packing area in another building. Of course, the blowing dust contaminated all the houses in the neighborhood. Alexa's calculations had revealed that the attic dust in those houses contained arsenic at levels ten thousand times higher than that thought to be toxic by the EPA.

"Woolfolk is just one example of many."

"Akbar, no one meant to harm anybody at Woolfolk. When they set up the conveyor belt there, no one knew any better. When they built the plant, people there were pleased because of the jobs. People living in the worst of those houses were bought out."

"You miss the point, Alexa. Think about West Dallas. That situation is probably closest to this one. There were percent levels of lead in the soil in West Dallas. It took years of effort by the West Dallas community to get anything to happen. The history of this sort of racism is pernicious. The West Dallas community was exposed to toxic levels of lead for fifty years." His voice rose, and she could sense his agitation. "The powers that be got away with it because the community was poor, black, and powerless."

"Akbar, you're worried about the placement of facilities in minority communities. You know why it happens—because the land is cheap there. That's the bottom line."

"You're saying it's just the economic realities that have put black people in this situation?"

"Exactly, Akbar."

"Then the government should have stepped in and stopped the construction of the polluting facility."

"It was the government that let them in, Akbar. Local government controls zoning. It's mostly jobs and economic growth, like I mentioned before."

"I understand what you're saying, Alexa. But what I'm saying is that we need a paradigm shift in the way we look at the environment. It's not good enough to find reasons or excuses anymore. Something has to change the mindset of the public. To be free of toxic hazards is a basic human right."

They were interrupted just then by the Reverend Smith.

"I got to lock up," he told them.

Alexa grinned.

"You got me pretty involved in that discussion, Akbar. Can I give you a ride back to your hotel? If my car won't start, at least you'll know how to fix it."

Alexa's Corolla started right up. They drove to the motel on Howell Mill Road in silence.

"What did you mean by a paradigm shift?" said Alexa when she stopped at a traffic light near the motel.

"Exactly that. We have to start looking at environmental protection in new ways. What values should we adopt for the urban landscape? You know why black people have not adopted the major environmental movements?"

"No," she said, playing along. "Why, Akbar?"

The light changed, and she drove into the motel parking lot.

"Because protecting people is more important than protecting animals. Environmental movements have always concentrated on the wilderness. Black people don't have a problem with that, except that the wilderness has been emphasized and the cities overlooked. Case in point—when they built the oil pipeline along the coast of California, they made a big detour inland so the pipeline went through the East L.A. barrio. The location was chosen to miss Ronald Reagan's ranch. The explanation the oil company gave to the displaced people from the barrio was to protect the marine life in case of a spill. Thing is, the pipeline was routed through the part of the barrio with the most people. The people in the barrio had a problem with the fish being more valuable than they were."

She was impatient while he spoke and tapped her foot.

"I thought about this, Akbar. The majority of the time, placement of facilities happens because of cheap land. It's the bottom line, as always."

"Yes, but who obtained the benefit of the pipeline? White people, black people, and Latinos. Why shouldn't the burden of the pipeline be shared equally? In the South especially, it's been black people who have born much more than their share of the burden of industrialization."

"Akbar, it's still not racism. It's only economics."

"Alexa, the government has secret liaisons with the polluters—even with an African American president. Who do you think finances political campaigns? The government has institutionalized racism around exposure to industrial toxins. The government can step in again on the side of justice. Those who use the resource should bear the burden."

"In a perfect world, you'd be correct, Akbar. But most people are trying to be fair. Most people are trying to do the right thing. I agree that there are some places to live that are more desirable than others. Where we live is sometimes luck and sometimes personal choice. If you don't like where you live—for whatever reason—then move."

"Don't you realize," Akbar countered, "how restricted black people are in their movements just by being black? They get extra scrutiny . . . redlining. Can a black man get a decent mortgage no matter how much he makes? Then there's the people who can't afford to move. We can argue about whether it's the government or the polluters later, but the circumstances of poor people's lives have forced them to live with this toxic legacy."

She started to speak, but he held his hand up to stop her.

"I spoke tonight, Alexa, about genocide. The government ignoring the plight of disenfranchised minorities is genocide!"

They had been parked for about ten minutes, still talking.

Alexa put a cool hand on Akbar's forearm.

"I'm enjoying our conversation, Akbar. Why don't we continue it inside. I'll buy you a drink. Something."

"I'm afraid as a Muslim I don't drink. But I would like to continue."

"You can have a ginger ale. C'mon."

She was out of the car and walking into the hotel with Akbar following.

The bar in the hotel was ratty with a frayed carpet. They seated themselves at a table in the corner. When no service was forthcoming, Alexa went to the bar and came back with a beer and a ginger ale.

"Alexa, there was one thing I was wondering about. Who is Jack Williams?"

"Was. He's dead now." The reminder of Jack Williams made her feel sad.

"Who was he?"

"Lawyer. Worked in the mayor's office. He was . . . well, we were on our way to becoming friends."

"He was connected to the church? The Reverend Watkins talked about him. If he were still alive, it seems I would have no place there."

Alexa looked up at him and smiled. She felt wistful. Thinking of Jack Williams made her wonder what might have been.

"What is it?" Akbar asked her.

"Jack was special to a lot of people. I didn't know about his connection to the church, but I think I remembered hearing that he grew up in Summerhill. He stayed close to his roots."

She sipped her beer.

"You know, Akbar, that would be so nice, to feel some connection to a place, the way Jack did. Do you have it? Do you really feel that Chicago is home? I don't know how I feel about Atlanta. Sometimes I feel like it's just a stop on the way."

"What was he like? Jack Williams?"

"Akbar, he's dead . . . why do you want to know?"

"I want to serve these poor children as well as Jack Williams would have. He's the model that everyone in that church tonight was holding me up to. I want to measure up."

"He was . . . well, quieter than you."

"Alexa, I have a fire in my belly. It's who I am."

"I know, but sometimes it's more effective to be quieter."

"The meek shall inherit the earth?"

"Something like that, Akbar."

"Did black people ask to be victims?" Alexa could hear the rage in his voice. "After all, who were the slaves in this country and who were the masters? Sure, Obama was elected, but very little else has changed."

"I know people of your race have had to fight for everything. Jack knew that too, but he was able to move past his feelings and fit in with society. I think he was in a position to accomplish the things you speak so eloquently about."

"Alexa, did his death increase his greatness?"

"People are aware that he left a hole in the world. Especially now with the children and their illness . . . he couldn't have died at a worse time. I think he would have done great things. Jack was ambitious, but he didn't forget where he came from." There was a lump in her throat. She squared her shoulders and leaned back from the table.

"So how did Jack Williams die?" he asked.

"You didn't see what was in the papers?"

"I've only seen the news on CNN in the morning up in my room."

"I found the body, but at the time I couldn't recognize him. He was murdered and dumped in a landfill sixty miles west of here."

She drank off the rest of her beer.

"Time for a pit stop. I'll be back," she said and got up.

A few minutes later, Alexa glided back to the table, elegant in the smoky darkness of the bar.

She smiled at Akbar when she sat down.

"There's one thing I've been wondering about, Akbar. What do you get out of all this?"

"Nothing for myself," he answered quickly. "What I want is to help my race."

"No, there's more to it. I heard what you said in the church tonight, but there's more."

He was silent. She waited for him to continue. When he didn't, she spoke.

"Okay, Akbar, I'll tell you about me first. Sure, I want to help these kids, but I also wanted the boost this has given my career. I haven't been a major player up till now, but the CDC put me on contract, and I've got their lab facilities to use whenever I want. I like the power I've got. Is that selfish?"

She reached across the table and squeezed him arm.

"Now, tell me about you," she said. "What do you want?"

He smiled and looked at the ceiling for a moment.

"I . . . I want to be the next leader of my race. Since Martin, there's been no one. No man or woman has had the charisma to bridge the gap for black people. Older folks still think they are owed something. I agree in a way and sympathize. Younger people, many of them anyway, want to be independent. But they can't because of the stereotype the black race has in this nation.

"Alexa, can't you feel the hunger in the land for someone to look up to? This is way past any racial differences. Both blacks and whites want inspiration. All of us have been so disappointed by those who claim to be leaders. They've been false leaders. I want to be the true spiritual leader, the people's inspiration for the future."

Even in the darkness, Alexa could see the overly bright look of excitement in his eyes, the hallmark of a zealot.

"Well, no one would accuse you of aiming too low, Akbar. You want to be the next prophet."

He stared at the glass of ginger ale in front of him and began to tear the damp napkin under his glass into little pieces.

"I haven't ever told that to anyone," he said.

"Akbar, it's a difficult goal to keep in perspective, I would think. It goes back to my original question. Are you doing this for those poor kids or for yourself? I don't think you honestly know the answer."

He hesitated before answering.

"You're right. I don't know."

He took a sip of ginger ale.

"So what do you want, Alexa? Really want? Beyond career success."

"I used to think I wanted exactly what I've got now—a great career. But now that I've got it, I realize there's more. What do I really want? This sounds crazy, but to love and to be loved."

"You've met someone?" he asked her.

"No, not really. It's just that lately there's a man who doesn't seem as interested as I am. I haven't told this to anyone either."

They were silent for several seconds.

"You and I both unloaded some secrets tonight," said Alexa. "I guess that makes us friends."

"We'll be in this together for a while, Alexa. I'm honored to be your friend."

She checked her watch.

"It's late, Akbar. I gotta go."

She walked around the table, placed her hands on his shoulders, and kissed his cheek. Then she walked out.

CHAPTER 18

FIRST DATE

Friday, October 20

When Bud and Christopher arrived home that night, Bud ordered pizza. He was exhausted. Since the meeting on Wednesday, he and Roscoe had made no progress finding any leads in the murder of Jack Williams. The Klan connection seemed just a coincidence.

It was really dumb of Alexa to have followed those two men and talked to them. If the children were being poisoned, she had done nothing to show that the men she followed—whoever they might be—were responsible. She had put herself in danger for nothing.

Bud's son interrupted his thoughts.

"Dad, it's the weekend. Can we go to the zoo on Sunday? Maybe that lady Alexa we met at the store could come with us? Please?"

"I don't know, Christopher. I know she was nice in the store, but she probably has other plans."

In response, Christopher walked to the kitchen and brought Bud the cordless phone.

"Okay, okay" said Bud, pulling out his wallet and looking for the card Alexa had given him.

"You know she likes you," said Christopher. Now both his son and his partner at work had told him that Alexa liked him.

"She was just being nice, Christopher, but I'll call her."

Bud dialed the number for Alexa's home, and she picked up on the third ring.

"I'm trying to reach Alexa Mason. This is Bud Prior."

"Oh, Bud, I'm so glad you called."

He didn't want to get into the whole poisoning issue with her again.

"Alexa, this is not related to any of my work, so please don't ask questions about that. You remember meeting my son, Christopher, at Trader Joe's?"

"Sure."

"We were wondering if Sunday you'd like to go to the zoo with us, my son and I."

"Of course, I do. What a great kid he is! I'd love to go to the zoo on Sunday with both of you."

Christopher had moved closer to Bud on the couch so he could hear the phone call.

"See, Dad. I told you," he whispered.

"Why don't I meet you there?" said Alexa.

"How about one o'clock?" said Bud. "East parking lot off Boulevard?"

"Sounds great, Bud. I'm looking forward to it."

Sunday, October 22

Yesterday had been cold—about 45 degrees—but this day was much warmer, and the mercury was pegging sixty.

Bud pulled his white truck into the lot and saw Alexa leaning against the back of her Corolla, looking great in jeans and a UGA sweatshirt. He pointed her out to Christopher.

"Hi, Alexa," Bud said when they had parked. "You remember Christopher."

"Of course I do."

Alexa squatted so she was face-to-face with Christopher.

The boy hugged her neck. "I'm so glad you came with us, Alexa," he said.

Bud smiled at her when she stood up and received a hug of his own.

Bud paid the admission for the three of them at the gate. "Where would you like to go first, Christopher?" he asked the boy when they were inside.

"I want to see the tigers."

The big cats were kept in large wooded paddocks surrounded by deep concrete moats separating them from the zoo-goers. The sign in front of the low wall indicated that the zoo's lone tiger was present, but the animal was nowhere to be seen.

Finally, the tiger came loping with easy grace from a door in a low building. The muscles in the striped shoulders rippled.

"There he is!" cried Christopher.

The tiger began to pace back and forth on the other side of the moat with a menacing air.

Bud looked over at Alexa as Christopher watched the tiger. Even dressed down, she looked terrific. As if she felt his attention, she turned, and they smiled at each other. She slipped her hand into his and squeezed.

"Willie B.," said Christopher looking up.

They walked slowly over to the primate house to catch a glimpse of the famous silver-back gorilla.

Willie B. was sitting in the corner of his cage slowly eating a banana.

"It's kind of a shame," said Alexa to Bud, "to keep these beautiful animals in cages. I know the zoo tries to treat them well, but there's something missing, some light not there in their eyes, and I think it's from being caged."

"I know what you mean, Alexa. Wild animals look different."

As they walked out of the primate house, Christopher hurried ahead of them.

"He's got lots of energy now," said Bud, "but he crashes at four o'clock or so."

"He's such a terrific kid," said Alexa. "I love his honesty, that he says what he thinks."

"Yeah," said Bud. "I don't want him to lose that honesty."

They ended up seeing about half the exhibits in the zoo before, true to Bud's prediction, Christopher got tired.

Bud found them a table in the Wild Planet Café, the zoo's main eatery. There was an outside patio, and each table was shaded by a large multicolored umbrella. Next door to the café was a playground.

Bud ordered lemonade for the three of them.

Christopher drank about half of his lemonade and asked to go to the playground.

"Go ahead," Bud smiled at his son.

"Christopher's such a great kid," said Alexa.

"He seems to really like you, Alexa."

"It's impossible not to like him back."

"I'm lucky to have him." Bud grinned. "But it's hard sometimes being a single parent."

Alexa idly stirred her lemonade. "I get chills just thinking of what a responsibility a kid must be. I mean, you take care of them all the way until . . . well, it never does stop, does it? If Christopher was forty and needed money or help, you'd give it to him, wouldn't you?"

"Of course, I would. How could you turn your children away? There's a whole biological thing that most people don't cop to. Kids are the way to keep your genes in the world. In a way, they make you immortal. Does that sound crazy?"

She laughed. As he looked in her eyes, Bud felt his throat tighten.

"I haven't felt that part about my genes yet, Bud. I always learn so much from you. I want to ask you something," she continued. "If I'm out of line, tell me. How does Christopher feel about his mother?"

"I don't think he remembers her. We only talked about it a little."

"Has he ever said he misses having a mom?"

"I think he must have some sense of loss. Alexa, I feel I've got to be careful about who I see, but Christopher was actually the one who picked you. He got me to call you to ask you to the zoo. I'm really glad he did." Bud looked at his lemonade and took a small sip.

As he put his glass down, he felt her hand on his, her small fingers wrapped around his.

"Bud, you remember when we met at the mayor's party? You shook my hand. I haven't forgotten how your hand felt." She blushed and looked down.

"Alexa, the biggest concern I've had with seeing any woman is Christopher, but with you, it wouldn't be a problem. He doesn't hug everybody."

She stood up from her chair, leaned toward him, and put her hands on his shoulders. Then she kissed him full on the lips, a kiss full of both love and longing.

Bud's heart fluttered, and he felt his toes curl. The kiss ended. She sat down and gazed into his eyes.

"Bud, you're a fine man and you've raised a beautiful son. We all have baggage."

"Both Christopher and Roscoe have told me they think you like me."

"Well, they're right," she said. She pushed her chair closer to his and took his hand. "Bud, the one thing I don't want is the kind of relationship my parents had. I think they stayed together out of convenience or fear of being alone. I think they felt trapped. Sometimes I get scared that I'll end up trapped like that as well. That's my baggage."

"Sandi, my wife, got leukemia when Christopher was two. I watched her shrink away to nothing before my eyes. I only took Christopher to the hospital twice, not near the end. Sandi didn't want him to remember her that way. I know he must feel some loss, but he never talks about it. I've asked him. I want him to have a woman in the house, to have him raised by a woman as well as me. But I also don't want to create problems for him."

"Oh, Bud, I'm so sorry for you." She kissed his hand.

Alexa put her head down. After a moment, he lifted her chin and saw that her cheeks were wet.

"It's okay," she said, wiping the tears with her fingers. "Just an old memory of my own." She grinned at him as Christopher came back to the table.

The boy threw himself into Bud's arms.

"Did you have fun today, Christopher?"

"I sure did, Dad. I'm hungry. Can we go eat?"

"It's getting on to six o'clock. Long time since lunch—right, Christopher? Where would you like to go?"

"Flying Biscuit, of course."

The Flying Biscuit was fast becoming an Atlanta tradition. The restaurant served an eclectic cuisine developed by the owner, April Moon. She opened the Candler Park restaurant in response to the growing homogenization of the Atlanta restaurant fare. Whenever Bud and Christopher wanted to celebrate, they went there.

The restaurant occupied two rooms on the corner of Clifton Road and McClendon Avenue. The decor was as eclectic as the food was delicious. The place had become an Atlanta legend.

The hostess showed Bud, Christopher, and Alexa to a table in the corner.

"This is our favorite place," Bud told her.

"I've read about it in the paper and *Atlanta Magazine*, but I've never made it over here."

"It's a treat," said Christopher.

"So, Christopher," said Alexa after they had ordered, "did you have fun at the zoo?"

"Yup. I like the zoo."

"What was your favorite animal?"

"The tiger, because of his stripes and because he hides a lot."

Bud smiled, watching them.

"I'm going to wash up," said Bud. "Christopher, you too? You'll excuse us, please, Alexa?"

"Sure."

When they were in the men's room, Bud leaned against the wall.

"You really like Alexa, don't you?"

"She's very cool, Dad. She likes kids—and you."

"I like her too, but we don't know what's going to happen. I guess what I'm saying is don't get too attached to her. Alexa is really nice, but I don't want you to really like her and then not be able to see her anymore."

"So you do like her, Dad?"

"Well, yeah, but I don't know her very well, and neither do you. I guess all I'm saying, son, is to take it easy. Just have fun."

"If you really started to like her, would she move in with us?"

"Let's not jump the gun, Christopher. I don't know how she feels."

"Are you kidding, Dad? I knew she liked you from that time in Starbucks, you know, when she kissed you."

"It's just not that easy. Liking someone, even falling in love, sometimes isn't enough. I don't want either of us to get too attached to Alexa and then feel hurt if she moves along."

"Dad, I haven't told you this, but I think I'd like a mom. I know you told me about my mom, but I really can't remember her. It makes me feel a little sad. Maybe Alexa could be like a mom?"

"We just gotta be careful, Christopher. It hurt me so much when your mom . . ." Bud couldn't finish for the lump in his throat. "Listen, wash up and go back to the table. I'll be there soon."

Bud watched his son go out the door. A single sob racked his chest when he thought of his wife.

My son is right, he thought. *It is time to move on.*

"You like dogs or cats?" he heard Alexa ask Christopher as he got back to the table.

"We've got an old cat, but I'd kinda like to get a dog."

"You know we talked about that, Christopher," said Bud. "Dogs need lots of attention."

"What's your favorite day of the week?" Alexa asked the boy.

"Friday, because I have the whole weekend to look forward to."

"Mine too, for the same reason. Fridays are just so full of promise."

The waitress took their order and brought drinks back.

"You ordered a hamburger," said Alexa. "I guess that means you like hamburgers better than hotdogs."

"That's right."

"What's your favorite candy bar?"

"Reeses, of course."

"Mine too."

Christopher was clearly enjoying the attention from Alexa.

When the food arrived, the burger Christopher ordered was way too big for him to pick up and eat.

"Christopher," asked Bud, "do you need me to help you with your food?"

"I'll do it," said Alexa. "Christopher, how about I cut it up into pieces small enough to eat? That way you can use a fork."

"Thanks," said Christopher, "but I'm usually a big enough boy to cut up my own food."

"Christopher," she said, "I think you're a big boy for knowing what you can or can't do. It's a big burger on a small plate."

Alexa took up the task of cutting Christopher's dinner into bite-sized pieces.

"Thank you, Alexa," said the boy when she was done.

"No problem." She shared a smile with Bud, and they all dug in.

Bud paid the check when the meal was done.

All three of them had ridden in Bud's truck from the zoo, squeezing into the front seat with Christopher in the middle.

"So, Alexa, you really like my dad?" Christopher asked her when they squeezed into the truck for the ride back to the zoo to retrieve Alexa's car.

"I do right now, Christopher." She blushed and giggled. "Thing is, grownups take a long time to get to know each other. Your dad and I are still getting to know each other. I hope he likes me too."

"Okay," said the boy, nodding his head slowly.

Bud concentrated on driving and did not look over at Alexa.

When they parked next to Alexa's Corolla at the zoo, Christopher leaned over and hugged her.

Alexa looked right at Bud as she hugged his son.

"I do know one thing, Christopher," she said. "You have a wonderful father and you're a very lucky boy." She kissed the top of his head.

"Christopher," Bud said, "can you wait here while I make sure Alexa gets to her car okay?"

"I'll be fine, Dad."

Bud's hand found hers as they walked away from the truck. She intertwined her fingers in his.

"Bud, I want to hug and kiss you, but not with your son watching. I meant what I said about you being a wonderful man."

"Oh, Alexa," said Bud, feeling dizzy with emotion.

She dropped his hand, turned to face him, and stood on tiptoe to whisper in his ear. "Call me. It's magic when I'm with you, but we need to see where this is going."

She planted a tiny kiss on Bud's cheek, as she had first done at Starbucks, skipped to her car, and exchanged a wave with Christopher.

Then she hopped in the car and drove off.

CHAPTER 19

IN BLACK AND WHITE

Monday, October 23

Bud showed the newspaper article to Roscoe when he got into work. Akbar had made the front page of the *Atlanta Journal*.

> **Black community tested: clergy plans march and vigil**
> by Gloria Conchita Ortiz
>
> It has been hard to escape the news of the tragedy of African American children being poisoned with lead. Currently, over thirty children are in Grady Hospital receiving treatment. Concerned clergymen from black churches throughout the Atlanta area plan a march from the Summerhill neighborhood to the state capitol followed by a candlelight vigil. The march will begin at 5:00 p.m. on Saturday, October 28.
>
> "The purpose of the march and vigil is to focus national attention on the plight of these unfortunate children," said Minister Akbar Muhammad of the Jihad for Justice, a Chicago group devoted to racial equality. Reverend Rufus Watkins of the Summerhill church near Grant Park indicated that the community does not know how to combat what he claims is an "obvious toxic assault" on black youth. Several environmental justice groups are also sponsoring the march, including the Southern Organizing Committee of Atlanta,

Save the People of Brunswick, and Jesus People Against Pollution of Columbia, MS. (See p. 3H, March)

"I sure wish Akbar hadn't done this," said Roscoe. Here's why." He turned the laptop on his desk toward Bud. "Take a look at this."

Bud started reading the webpage. The prominent banner at the top bore both the Stars'n'Bars and several swastikas.

Attention all members:

The nigros have claimed that many of their young in Atlanta are being poisoned, lead-poisoned. The Jew York Times and the Atlanta newspapers both claim the same thing. The nigros say that their young are being brain-damaged by lead.

We of the Southern Mystic Knights know that nigros have very little brain to damage. Certainly, nigros are good at sports where little brain power is needed, but that is the only thing they are good at in the modern world.

The Southern Mystic Knights have learned that the nigros will stage a protest at the Georgia State Capitol in Atlanta.

What are we to do, my robed and hooded brethren? I say the Southern Mystic Knights and all others within the Invisible Empire of the Ku Klux Klan should attend a rally at the same place and the same time. Let us give the Jews in the media something to talk and write about.

The nigro protest is to be held at the capitol on Saturday, October 28, 5:00 p.m. That afternoon all Knights of the Klan who wish to send a message to the nigros, the media, and our government wear their robes and meet at the old Atlanta-Fulton County Stadium parking lot for a march to the capitol. A march permit from the city has been applied for. Once that permit is in hand, there is nothing the nigro government of Atlanta can do about us being there. Join us in this first important step to liberate Atlanta from the control of the lazy, whining nigros.

Knights of the Invisible Empire, arise!

Chapter 20

Hate Crimes

Tuesday, October 24

Christopher had a sore throat and was running a fever. Bud managed to get a doctor's appointment at 9:30. After waiting to see the doctor, waiting at the drug store for the necessary prescriptions, and then going home to wait for the sitter to arrive, Bud didn't get into the office until after eleven o'clock.

Roscoe was waiting for him.

"Bud, you seen the news yet?"

"Not today, Roscoe. Christopher's been sick. I took him to the doctor."

"It's starting to hit the fan about these poisonings. In response to the protest organized by Akbar and the black clergy, yesterday Atlanta City Hall got a request for a march permit from the Klan. Supposed to happen on the same day. Klan march also ends at the capitol—at the same time."

"Any way the Klan permit can be denied?"

"Well, you know, they tried that once before. The ACLU acting on behalf of the Klan has sued other cities. You know, free speech. The Klan got to hold the march. Strange bedfellows."

"So Atlanta doesn't want to fight that same battle?"

"That's right, but they're thinking about making a case for denying both permits as a public welfare issue."

"Then the city will piss off both groups."

"Yeah, but they figure it's better than a riot."

"I imagine we'll be there if it happens."

"Bud, plan on it happening and plan on being there. I think the courts will see it as a free speech issue for both sides. The FBI, the city cops, state troopers, and a National Guard battalion will be there. It'll be the most heavily guarded event in Atlanta since the Olympics."

After Bud took care of the immediate paperwork on his desk, he and Roscoe went out to get coffee at about 11:30.

It was a beautiful day, warm and sunny. They decided to walk north toward Five Points and hit the Starbucks near Woodruff Park.

"We got three things working right now as I see it," said Bud when they had gotten their coffee and secured an outside table. "There's this rally next weekend, there's the murder of Jack Williams, and there're these lead poisonings. I feel like we're behind the curve everywhere."

"Bud, I can't escape the feeling that the three are related. That makes it a bigger case and harder to understand, but it also means that if we push ahead on one, we push on all three."

"I got that feeling too, Roscoe—I mean about the three of them being connected. I think we should split up. I'll go back to the landfill in Cedartown, ask around. I'll also try to spend some time figuring out the last few hours of Jack Williams's life."

"Fine. I'll work on the poisonings. We have to find out where that fill dirt came from. I'll talk to each of the churches where kids have been poisoned."

Bud took a sip of his coffee.

"Ugh, legwork," he said to no one in particular.

"Good police work always comes down to that, doesn't it, Bud?"

Bud's first stop in Cedartown was the landfill. The foreman told him that the Klan hadn't shown up again since the day they found Jack Williams's body. Bud figured he might as well talk to Melanie Groover while he was there. Maybe she had some more information.

Bud arrived at the Groover place around 1:30. It was a beautiful day, the sun warm enough to take the chill out of the wind. Melanie Groover was sitting outside in a canvas beach chair, intermittently reading and watching her daughters play.

"Ms. Groover, I'm Sergeant Bud Prior, working for the FBI. Remember I came to see you before?"

"Yes, I remember. Hello, Sergeant."

"I want to ask you some more questions about Jimmy Ray. When did you last see him?"

"He came home last night and left again real early this morning. Since he got that job in Atlanta, I don't see him much. He has to get up so early, some nights he calls me an' jus' stays in Atlanta. He can usually find a place with one of the guys at work."

"You expect to see him tonight?"

"I don't know, Sergeant. I can't tell what he'll do until he either shows up or calls."

"Has Jimmy talked about his new job?"

"He likes it. At least, the pay's better. I know he hates commuting, but, Lordy, I sure would too."

Bud was at a loss for what else to ask her. Melanie Groover would not purposely incriminate her husband—her meal ticket—and she knew little of his activities.

"Could I look around the house, Ms. Groover?"

"Well, I dunno, Sergeant. What are you looking for?"

He stared at her a moment in silence.

"You haven't noticed anything different about Jimmy Ray, have you, Ms. Groover?"

She hesitated and sniffed.

"I ain't seen him enough to notice," was her reply.

"No," said Bud, "I guess not."

They looked at each other for a long moment. She started to cry.

Bud felt uncomfortable, but he made no move toward his truck. Melanie did not ask him to leave.

"What is it?" he said at last.

"It's . . . it's just I never get to see Jimmy anymore. The only thing tells me I'm married is these two kids and this ring. He don't do nothin' 'round this place. Never did. Before, when he worked at the landfill, well, least I saw him. Now I never even see him."

There was nothing Bud could say.

Bud had been staring at Melanie Groover for a full minute. She was still sniffling when one of the girls fell over and began to cry. Melanie wiped her nose on the back of her hand and picked up the girl.

"Watch Kelly, please," she said and went into the mobile home.

She came out a couple of minutes later.

"Ms. Groover," said Bud, "I sense you're having difficulty. You should know that by law, a wife can't incriminate her husband. You don't have to reveal anything you don't want to, and you can't be made to talk."

She rocked the baby and stared up at the sky.

"Sergeant," she said, "I think I'd like you to leave now. I need to be by myself."

"That's fine, Ms. Groover."

She picked up both girls and went into the mobile home.

Bud was about to get in his truck and drive away when he noticed a rip in the skirting of the mobile home. Sunlight shone into the rip. Inside the skirting he saw a flash of white. It was in plain sight so he didn't need a warrant.

Bud walked over, lifted the skirting, and pulled out some shiny white cloth. He held it up—it was a Klan robe. On the front were some dark brown stains.

Bud put the robe into a clean garbage bag he kept in his truck.

He looked at his watch. There would be just enough time to get back to Atlanta and pick up Christopher at day care. He could hit the foundry tomorrow.

That afternoon, Roscoe called Alexa and asked to come to her office.

"Ms. Mason, I need to know about the lead in the playgrounds. I want to see how you traced the source of this lead. You said at that meeting the other night that you know where the lead came from."

"I said I *thought* I knew where it came from. I'm not 100 percent sure."

"Fine," he said, blowing off her scientist's reluctance to commit to absolute certainty. "I'll be there soon, and I want to know your thoughts."

"I've got some confusing facts, Agent Harriman," she told him when he arrived. "Look, if we're going to spend the afternoon looking at pages of numbers, why don't you call me Alexa, and I'll call you . . ."

"Roscoe."

"Roscoe, would you like some coffee?"

"Sure. Be great."

Alexa fixed them a cup each and opened two reports on the large table in her office—the foundry site investigation and her report to the CDC about lead in the church playgrounds.

"In most of the playgrounds," she began, "well, it's pretty clear the dirt came from Seitzman's Foundry. Remember the disappearing dump truck?"

"Don't go there," Roscoe told her.

Alexa was still miffed at the FBI's seeming refusal to look into the men who had taken the dump truck, but she said nothing. She flipped pages in both reports until two tables of numbers were shown.

"Look, the lead levels from this area of the foundry site and the playground by the church on Spink Street were both very high. The foundry is the only place I know that has lead levels that high. I got further confirmation from the anions."

"Anions?"

"Jargon. I'm sorry. Anions are the chemicals that combine with lead in the soil, sulfate, chloride, stuff like that. If the anions are similar, then the soil probably came from the same place. The anions are also pretty much identical. You can see from these columns here," she said, pointing to the tables.

"Too many numbers there," said Roscoe. "I guess I'm not used to looking at that many."

"When you called, I tried to think of a way to make this simple. There really isn't one."

"Look. Shut these books, Alexa. I had more than enough of this stuff in school. Tell me in words."

"Okay. Let me get my map with all the churches marked on it."

Alexa unfolded an Atlanta map. She had drawn circles around each of the churches with a yellow highlighter.

"The churches here, here, here, here, here, here, here, here, and here," she said, pointing at the map with a pencil, "have dirt that looks like it came straight from the foundry site. These two sites," pointing again, "are different. I don't know why."

"One of the one's that's different is the Summerhill church, right?"

"That's right, Roscoe. The soil had real high lead, but the anions were different and there were other toxic metals. I don't know what to make of it."

"Alexa, all those churches are close to the foundry site, except for Summerhill and that other one. In a way, it's consistent with your idea that the lead came from the foundry."

"I guess I need to spend some more time with this and figure out if the lead in these two churches is similar enough to the lead at the foundry and also where the other metals came from. It may be that the foundry soil was mixed with some other soil, but that's a guess."

The other thing Roscoe knew he could do was to check on the sources of the fill dirt. They had already questioned the ministers of the churches that the poisoned kids had attended, and every church had built new playgrounds or refurbished an old one during the latter part of the summer in time for school. All of them had received donated fill dirt.

Roscoe parked the government sedan by the playground at the Summerhill Primitive Missionary Baptist Tabernacle. Reverend Watkins opened the front door of the church and waved him in before he turned the car off.

Watkins ushered him into the fellowship hall, and they sat in a couple of the folding chairs.

"So who did you call for the fill dirt?" asked Roscoe after the two had made their greetings.

"A number I got off a poster stapled to a telephone pole."

"Can you show me where?"

"Sure. We can walk there."

The telephone pole, a quarter mile away at the corner of Sydney and Connally Streets, was covered with staples, testament to the many handbills and advertisements that had been posted there at one time or another.

"That's where it was," said Watkins. "Had them tabs with numbers for folks to be tearin' off."

"I know what you mean. Do you still have the number?"

"If I do, it's on my desk," replied Watkins.

When they got back to the church, the number was nowhere to be found.

Roscoe then drove to the Old Bolton Baptist Church Sanctuary on Bolton Road at Spink Street. A thin dark-skinned man about fifty years old greeted him.

"Reverend Jasper?"

"Yes," said the man. "That's me."

"I'm Special Agent Roscoe Harriman of the FBI's hate crimes unit. We're investigating the lead poisoning. I was at the meeting last Wednesday where Akbar Muhammad and Alexa Mason spoke."

"I remember it well."

"Reverend Jasper, I know two of the affected children were associated with this church."

"That's right."

"Did you get any fill dirt this summer?"

"Yes, we did. I call this number I found on a poster. I remember when the dirt arrived; it was in a dump truck driven by two raggedy-assed white boys. They was real polite though. One guy had blond hair, ponytail, wore a Metallica T-shirt. Other guy was sorta dumpy, looked like a redneck, you know what I mean. They dumped the dirt on the playground. We spread it out later."

"Could you identify them if you saw them again?"

"I sure could."

"That phone number you called, Reverend. Do you still have it?"

"Let me see."

He ushered Roscoe into his office and rummaged through a collection of bills and other papers in a bowl.

"Here it is!"

Roscoe copied the number into his notebook, thanked the man, and left.

At the next four churches, Roscoe collected different phone numbers. It seemed like the phone numbers would not be too much of a lead.

He parked the government car and dialed the first number on his cell phone. It was a pager. Roscoe didn't bother to leave a number.

The second number was a digital pager, giving him a generic message from something called Acme Services. The third and fourth numbers were answering machines with identical generic greetings: "Hello. No one can take your call right now. Please leave a message and a way to get back to you."

The fifth number was another pager.

He drove back to the Russell building to try to find the numbers in the blue book, the reverse phone directory.

The blue book did tell him that the billing address for all five numbers was a post office box in the Bolton Road Post Office. He realized he could stake out the post office for days and no one would show up. It was a dead end.

Wednesday, October 25

Bud drove up to the foundry. He wanted another word with Waters, Jimmy Ray's boss.

Torres, the foreman, called Waters into the construction trailer at the site.

Bud was surprised at how thin the man was up close, almost skeletal. His head was shadowed with dark stubble above slitted eyes.

"Claude Waters, right?" Bud began the interview.

"That's right."

"I think one of the men you hired is in the Ku Klux Klan."

"Sergeant Prior, I don't know anything about it. I don't check out their politics. I just need to know if they can drive heavy equipment and can get to work on time. I can get 'em HazMat training if they need it. Who is it? Just out of curiosity."

"Jimmy Ray Groover. You didn't know, huh?"

"Why would I know?"

Bud wondered how much to tell the man. Except for his shaved head and dour demeanor, Waters seemed pretty normal. A little quiet, taciturn, but that was all.

Bud realized that in his two previous interviews with Waters, the man had revealed almost nothing about himself.

"Mr. Waters, is there any way the contaminated soil could be taken from the site?"

"Well, sure. They're taking it to Emelle, Alabama, by the truckload. I figure it gets to Emelle, but I don't follow the trucks. My job here is with the heavy equipment."

"Emelle?"

"It's a town in Alabama with a big hazardous waste landfill. But that ain't what you're talkin' about, is it?"

"No, I think someone's stealing this soil for their own use."

"That wouldn't be too smart," said Claude.

"No, but I get the sense that maybe it's an inside job. You got any insight for me?"

"They lock the gates every night. I don't know who could get in here. You should check with Torres about who has keys. During the day, access is controlled too. It used to be freer access, but since the lead poisonings hit the news . . . Fact is, you likely couldn't even go back there—you ain't had HazMat training."

"So you don't think there's any way I could look around the site?"

"I really don't care what you do, but it's not up to me. You gotta check with Torres."

When Bud asked, Torres told him no way, not without the training.

Chapter 21

The Scientist and the Prophet

Thursday, October 26

Since their date at the zoo, Bud and Alexa talked on the phone daily. Bud usually called Alexa around eleven in the morning. Neither of them had been able to get free for lunch the entire week. They hadn't seen each other in person since Sunday at the zoo.

Today he called her as soon as he got into the office.

"Oh, hey, Bud," said Alexa after she recognized his voice on the phone.

"You see the paper today, Alexa?"

"Nope."

"Nice article about you in the Living section. They also got an article about Akbar."

The Living section of the *Atlanta Journal Constitution* that day featured articles on both Akbar Muhammad and Alexa, their backgrounds and how each came to be involved with the children's lead poisoning.

"I'll get a copy, Bud."

"I still can't make lunch today. I hate that. There're just too many things to check on before the march and the rally. You know the city hasn't denied either permit—Akbar's or the Klan's."

"I understand. Look, tomorrow's Friday. Maybe you'll get it all done by tomorrow. Then we can have lunch."

"I'm looking at my calendar. That looks like it might be a go. I'm planning on it for now."

"I hope so, Bud."

"Go read the paper."
"Call me later if you've got time."

Alexa settled in her office chair with the paper and started reading.

Environmental scientist takes on lead poisoning
by Gloria Conchita Ortiz

Alexa Mason worries about the children who have been poisoned with lead. Anyone watching the news or reading the paper could not escape knowing about the tragedy of these children. Alexa Mason knows firsthand.

Ms. Mason received a degree in environmental health science from the University of Georgia five years ago. It didn't take her long to establish her own business. This fall she discovered the first child who had been poisoned by lead.

"The saddest part of it is what will become of these children," Ms. Mason commented in a recent interview. (see Scientist, p. 3C)

Alexa didn't find the rest of the article that interesting, although she came off well in Ortiz's terse prose. She started reading the piece on Akbar.

Justice through non-violence
by Gloria Conchita Ortiz

Minister Akbar Muhammad has devoted his life to the quest for racial and environmental justice. Minister Muhammad, a descendant of the late Wallace Fard Muhammad who founded the Nation of Islam, leads a Chicago organization called the Jihad for Justice. He has come to Atlanta to champion the plight of the lead-poisoned children.

"These poor children's lives must be put back together," said Muhammad, "but they can serve a higher purpose as well. These children can focus the nation's attention on the plight of the poor and people of color regarding toxic waste. Toxic waste is the unfortunate legacy of industrialization. Poor people, predominantly African Americans, bear most of the burden of this legacy but share few of the advantages of our technological society."

On Saturday, Minister Muhammad has organized a march and a rally for concerned citizens, clergy, and anyone else interested. The purpose of the march and rally is to publicize the children so that, in the hopefully prophetic words of Minister Muhammad, "something this terrible never happens again."

The march will begin at 4:00 p.m. this Saturday at the Summerhill Primitive Missionary Baptist Tabernacle on Connally Street near Turner Field. The march will proceed to the state capitol where the rally will be held. (see Prophet, p. 3C)

Before turning to the inside page, Alexa examined both photographs. The one of her was flattering but not striking. Akbar's photo showed him standing in front on the Summerhill Primitive Missionary Baptist Tabernacle. The state capitol was in the background. The photographer had shot him from a low angle, and with his dreadlocks and polished bronze features, Akbar looker archetypal, larger than life.

Chapter 22

Lunch Interrupted

Friday, October 27

Bud called Alexa at nine that morning. He asked if they could meet at Giuseppe's, an Italian place in Underground Atlanta.

They both walked up at the stroke of 11:30, squeezed each other's hands, and she kissed him from the tips of her toes.

The restaurant was small and dark. The maître d' showed them to a booth in the back corner. Bud ordered wine for them and then turned to the menu.

"I've never been here before, Bud. What a terrific place. It's perfect!"

They talked about the march scheduled for the following day and the preparation the police had made. To Alexa, the show of force the police were planning seemed more than enough to quell any disturbance.

"All the same," Bud told her, "I know I can't tell you what to do, but I wish you'd stay away. I'd feel better. The police can't do everything, and it's, well . . . a volatile situation."

"Bud, I've got to be there. The Reverend Watkins has asked me to speak again. I can't just turn away from all those poor children."

Bud rubbed his jaw thoughtfully.

"I don't guess you can skip it. Alexa, just be super careful tomorrow. Make sure one of the cops is near you at all times."

"Don't worry, Bud."

She took another sip of wine and stared at him, smiling.

"So I've got nothing happening this afternoon. How about you, Bud?"

Bud felt her bare foot on his calf, his knee, and then high on the inside of his thigh.

As Alexa caressed him with her foot, Bud felt the blood pound in his temples.

"Oh, Alexa."

As if they were already seasoned lovers, her toe found his most sensitive spot, and Bud inhaled sharply.

"I've got to pick Christopher up at four. Nothing until then."

"Bud, I sure like the old Biltmore Hotel. You know, on Fifth Street. They've got rooms with Jacuzzi baths."

She gave him one final rub with her foot.

Bud raised his hand to summon the waiter.

"Check, please."

He left money on the table, and they got up to leave. Bud reached for her hand. Just as they touched, his cell phone rang.

He looked at the screen.

"I gotta take this call, Alexa. It's Roscoe."

He opened the phone and listened.

"Bud, it's me," said Roscoe. "You remember Mrs. Groover, uh, Melanie?"

"Yeah. I just saw her this week."

"Well, she's here now, and she's got some tale about her husband and the march tomorrow. You need to hear it."

"Roscoe, it's really not the best time."

"Hey, Bud, I can't help it that she came in. She's asking for you specifically. Won't tell me anything. She says she knows something about the march tomorrow, but she'll only tell you."

"I'll be there in half an hour, Roscoe."

He squeezed his eyes shut a moment.

"Oh, Alexa. I'm so sorry."

Alexa hugged him again, holding herself against him. He felt the warmth at the base of her belly against his leg, and he thought for the briefest moment of calling Roscoe back.

"Don't worry, Bud," she said as she pushed away from him. "You're a man—a standup guy. You do what you say you'll do. You and I . . . well, it wasn't supposed to happen today." She pulled him close and whispered, "It'll be even better when it finally does happen."

"Thanks for understanding, Alexa."

She stepped away, still holding his hand.

"Now you go do whatever you need to do and rest assured I will be extra careful tomorrow. You be careful tomorrow too. I'm not done getting to know you, Bud Prior."

She leaned and kissed his cheek.

Melanie Groover, her two girls, and another woman were sitting in the cramped waiting room outside the FBI bullpen of the fourth floor of the Russell Building.

"Hello, Ms. Groover," said Bud when he walked in. "Agent Harriman said you wanted to see me. I'm sorry I wasn't here when you arrived."

"Christy, could you watch the girls?" asked Melanie.

"Sure," said the other woman.

"Would you please come in here?" said Bud, pointing toward an interview room.

"It's private?" asked Melanie.

"Sure is," said Bud.

He held open the door and ushered her into one of the small spare interrogation rooms.

"Ms. Groover, I take it this is about your husband."

"Yes. He came home las' night. It was something he said while we was eating."

Melanie hesitated.

"Go on," he prompted her.

"Jimmy Ray was talkin' las' night 'bout goin' to this march. You know, the uh . . . negroes at the capitol."

"Did he say why he was going?"

"There's a rumor where he works. You know, those kids that have been lead poisoned. The rumor is the lead came from that foundry site where he works. He said a bunch of the guys are gonna show up to let people know it wasn't them."

"So Jimmy Ray's going to the march to support the children?" Bud said incredulously. "Why did he tell you anything at all, Ms. Groover?"

"The time I saw him before that, I told him he was gonna have to start talking to me if we was gonna stay together. I can't stand livin' like this, wonderin' all the time whether what he says is a lie. You know when I asked you to leave the other day? Well, I seen what you found. I can't stop thinking that Jimmy Ray lied to me about the Klan."

She forced the last sentence out hurriedly and then began to cry.

"Ms. Groover," persisted Bud, "why do you think he's really going to the march?"

"God, I dunno. If he's goin' as part of the Klan, I'm done with him. I called my momma this mornin' an' talked about it. I ain't gonna raise my girls up to hate people. It ain't right. I'll leave him before I see my girls grow up like that."

"Ms. Groover, I'll be right back," he told her.

"So what'd she say?" asked Roscoe outside the room.

"She watched me find that Klan robe the other day. She gave Jimmy Ray an ultimatum. He told her he was going to the march as a crew from the foundry supporting the poisoned children."

"Yeah, right," boomed Roscoe, his voice dripping with sarcasm.

"My thoughts exactly. Still, Melanie and the kids might be in danger. She should stay away from Jimmy Ray. We need to watch him ourselves tomorrow."

Bud went back into the interview room.

"Ms. Groover, do you have a place to go? You mentioned possibly staying at your mother's. Would you and your girls be safe there?"

"I could go there. I was worried about going back home after this."

"Please stay with your mother."

Bud ushered the two women and Melanie's two girls out to their car parked in the visitor's lot behind the Richard Russell building.

When he got back inside, Roscoe had another idea to ponder.

"Bud, you wondered if Jimmy Ray had anything to do with Jack Williams's murder. Where's that going?"

"Well, we don't have lab work on the Klan robe back yet, but the stains did look like blood."

"Bud, he could be dangerous tomorrow. If he already killed a man, stepped over the line before, we don't know what he could do tomorrow."

Chapter 23

The March

Saturday, October 28

The day of the march, Akbar brought in pizza for a late lunch at the Summerhill Primitive Missionary Baptist Tabernacle. The Reverend Watkins had invited the other clergy to the church to discuss strategy for the march.

Four of the clergy wanted to speak at the rally. They decided that the Reverend Watkins would speak first, followed by Alexa. Akbar would introduce the other ministers, who promised to be brief, and then he would speak himself.

People started to arrive at 3:00 in the afternoon. By four, the police were directing the overflowing crowd to assemble around the Olympic warm-up track at the nearby Cheney Stadium.

Akbar could barely contain his excitement. The crowd was mixed, mostly black with a handful of whites. Many of the marchers carried signs that read Save the Children, End Environmental Racism, or a similar message.

At 4:30, Congressman John Lewis arrived. He shook hands all round and indicated that he brought greetings from President Obama, who would be unable to attend for security reasons. Camera crews from CNN, Fox News, and MSNBC arrived and set up their gear.

The Atlanta Police motorcycle squad organized the marchers in a line stretching south on Connelly Street all the way to Georgia Avenue.

Akbar, Congressman Lewis, the Reverend Watkins, and Alexa took their places at the head of the march.

A few minutes before five, the marchers grew silent. One of the cops handed Akbar a bullhorn.

"We are gathered here today," he began, multiple echoes of his amplified voice stirring the crowd, "not only to right a great wrong but to inform the world of this wrong. Let the world judge the rightness or wrongness of what has happened."

A low rumble came from scattered parts of the crowd of marchers. The rumble grew in both volume and intensity until it seemed the voice of a multitude.

Akbar took his place at the head of the march. He linked arms with Congressman Lewis and the Reverend Watkins and began to walk north toward Fulton Street. He noted with satisfaction that news cameras had recorded the start of the march.

Bud had reviewed the plan the APD had created for managing the march. APD was out in force. All police leave had been cancelled, and everyone from the rank of major on down was working the rally. Fulton County had supplied their share of uniforms, and volunteer cops from Cobb and Dekalb Counties were also present. All told, there were 850 uniforms at the rally, and the mayor also had the National Guard standing by.

APD had assigned its biggest and toughest cops to stay between the Klan and the marchers.

"They're gonna stay on the Klan like white on rice," Bud joked to Roscoe.

"More like stink on shit, which is what the Klan is," retorted Roscoe grimly.

Bud and Roscoe stayed on the capitol grounds. Twenty FBI men were spread around the capitol area and were in constant touch by their earplug radios.

Bud looked for Alexa as soon as he heard the marchers singing. His heart sank when he saw her in the first row of the march. In spite of his warnings, he knew she had to show her face prominently.

Bud began to get a bad feeling and tried to comfort himself with the sight of at least a hundred uniformed cops accompanying the march.

The marchers assembled on the capitol grounds, and he watched Alexa follow the Reverend Watkins, Akbar, and Congressman Lewis toward the podium.

Alexa smiled at Bud when he caught her eye, and she shyly waved to him with one finger. He beckoned her over and they held hands.

"Bud, they've got plans for me to speak. Not for long. I'll say what I said at the church meeting but shorter." She looked at the ground and squeezed his hand. "I'm gonna be on national TV."

Bud squeezed her hand back. Alexa was staring at the podium. For no specific reason, he was suddenly frightened for her.

"Be careful, Alexa."

"No sweat, Bud. Look at all these cops."

The large crowd on the capitol grounds was noisy until the Reverend Watkins stood at the podium with his arms raised.

"My friends, we all know the sad truth why we are here today," he began.

A murmur of assent rose from the crowd, and he let it die out before he continued.

"Several people will talk to you today, but the man most responsible for us being here is Minister Akbar Muhammad of the Jihad for Justice." Watkins turned and motioned for Akbar to stand and receive the applause of the crowd. "Minister Muhammad will speak later."

Alexa watched Akbar smile to himself as he sat down.

Watkins droned on for a few more minutes and then gave way to a short perfunctory address by Congressman Lewis.

When the congressman sat down, Watkins motioned to Alexa.

She moistened her lips self-consciously as she walked to the podium. She turned a moment and smiled at Akbar for reassurance. He clenched his fist in a gesture of encouragement.

Standing at the microphone, Alexa found Bud at the edge of the crowd and smiled at him as well.

"Good people, ladies and gentlemen," she began, "I was dismayed—no, I was horrified—when, several weeks ago, I discovered that a child, a young boy attending day care at Reverend Watkins's church, had lead poisoning. I'm sure you know how damaging lead is to children. For many years,

A Toxic Assault

health agencies, both private and public, have tried to find ways to limit children's exposure to lead.

"I studied the situation more closely, and I was even more troubled to learn that the boy had likely become poisoned from playing on a newly built playground. There were toxic levels of lead in the dirt at the playground."

At these words, a collective gasp emerged from the crowd.

Alexa cast her eyes around the capitol grounds and was energized by the crowd's rapt attention. Then she looked to the south on Courtland Street and saw the advancing white robes. Her emotion quickly turned to trepidation and then outrage. She resolved to get her message out.

"Our task today is not to wonder how dangerous levels of lead came to be in our playgrounds, but what can be done for the poor children and what we, as a nation, can do to make sure a tragedy like this never occurs again."

There was scattered applause from the crowd. To her right, Alexa saw the sea of white robes straining against the line of Atlanta cops holding them back. She noticed her hands were shaking. Bud had told her the Klan would be there, but she didn't think it would be so frightening.

"It ain't the lead, lady!" came a shout from the group of Klansmen. "It's just that niggers are stupid."

Alexa ignored the taunt and the scattered shouts of "nigger lover."

"I found that the children were indeed affected by lead. Where the lead came from was simple to discover."

When she paused, a roar went up from the Klan. It was loud enough to drown her out, even with the microphone.

"We have to prevent any more children from being affected."

"How can you say that what you're callin' brain damage just ain't the natural state o' the nigger?" cried a single voice from the white-robed mob.

"This won't happen again," she said. "All the children in Atlanta will be tested. We will make sure that no other children will be affected."

"So how're ya gonna pay for all this testin'?" asked the Klansman. "My tax money?"

Alexa's eyes flashed a deeper blue, showing her anger.

"We owe these children a decent life! That's all I have to say."

The crowd was silent for a moment. Then a cheer rose up from the marchers, and simultaneously, a roar erupted from the Klan. The white-robed mob surged forward but were held back by the line of police.

Alexa glared at the Klansman who had interrupted her, then turned and went to her seat.

"You shut them up, Alexa," said Akbar. "It was smart not to address that man directly. When he first interrupted, I didn't know what you would do. I don't think anyone could have handled it better than you."

"Maybe you, Akbar, but thanks for saying so. I was scared, but I was also angry."

"It didn't show. You were wonderful."

The Reverend Watkins was speaking again, introducing Akbar, who stood and walked to the podium. The people who were there for the children were respectfully silent. The Klan roared its hatred.

As Akbar walked to the podium, Alexa noticed the sharp demarcation in the sea of faces in front of him. On the right and in front of her, most faces were black. To the left, the robed Klansmen were like a white stain.

The police kept the Klan near the statue of Herman Talmadge, the late Georgia senator who kept his seat largely due to his racism.

"My friends," Akbar began, "my fellow men and women in the struggle, we gather here today to mourn these poor children's lives. Some of them may be permanently affected, rendered unable to function in society because of this toxic assault.

"Who will take care of the children? Who will ensure they get the services and benefits they need to get the most out of their meager and damaged lives? Who will try to make things right for them? Who will make them whole?"

There was applause from the crowd of marchers. The Klan was silent, but she saw many of them spit on the ground.

"Another group has chosen to join us here today. A group who has expressed nothing but hatred for us based on the color of our skin.

"I speak to both groups. The races can live together without strife. In fact, God wishes the races to coexist in harmony, to work together, and to love each other as fellow human beings."

The crowd fell silent.

"We know what happened to these poor children, and as Ms. Alexa Mason told us in such an eloquent way, there is great resolve to prevent the same fate from befalling other children.

"The children are a symbol for the most secret yet most pernicious form of racism our country has experienced—environmental racism. How could anyone deny that the children have suffered from this toxic assault—a criminal assault?

"It is the same everywhere in America. People of color are being forced to endure dirtier air, dirtier water, and worse living conditions."

At this, another spontaneous cheer broke from the crowd of marchers, and a roar of dissent from the Klan.

"I speak to you as well," Akbar continued, gesturing toward the Klan. "Toxic facilities are always sited in disadvantaged neighborhoods. The reason given is cheap land. But, think through this with me. Who benefits from our society's industrialization, and who bears the burden of its toxic legacy?"

He paused and surveyed the largely silent crowd.

"Poor people—that's who," Akbar answered his own question. "People of all colors—white, black, brown, and yellow, those who are without franchise in the halls of power and those who have been and continue to be excluded from our society's legislative and decision-making process.

"It is time for poor people, for black people, for white people, and for people of all colors to take a seat at the table. It is time for our voices to be heard.

"Our government has begun to listen to us, but listen is all they do. There has been nothing truly substantive done on our behalf. And still, the toxic assault on our race continues—not an overt assault like the one perpetrated on these poor children, but a subtle assault, hidden just below the surface yet no less harmful. Whenever a toxic facility is located in a community, we are assaulted. Whenever a neighborhood, urban or rural, becomes an illegal dump and the government does nothing, we are assaulted. Whenever jobs are unsafe because of toxic chemicals, jobs held by people who need those jobs to survive, again we are assaulted.

"So I ask you, where and when will it stop?

"I answer my own question. The toxic assault on the poor and the disenfranchised will stop right here and right now. It will stop because the American people are good. Even with all our problems, the people know right from wrong; they remain good people. And good people know right from wrong."

Alexa pondered his words, feeling the emotion, the righteous power he brought against the hatred of the Klan.

As Akbar paused, Alexa looked out at the crowd. She felt a sudden chill and shuddered even though the coming night hadn't yet chilled the air.

During the pause, the crowd was silent, even the Klan. Alexa heard a whistling sound, and she turned to see the Klan surge forward pulling ax handles from beneath their robes.

Bud was standing near the northwest corner of the capitol grounds. He had a clear view of the podium, a hundred yards away, where Akbar exhorted the throng. He watched the police hold back the Klan and tapped Roscoe on the shoulder to show him.

"Don't worry, Bud. If those pointy heads get too rowdy, APD'll start making arrests," Roscoe told him.

The biggest Atlanta cop was positioned to hold back the front of the white-robed mob. He had linked arms with two other policemen in a bulwark against the racists. As Akbar paused in his speech, the big cop's head exploded soundlessly in a spray of blood and bone. Bud watched open-mouthed as the Klan surged forward toward Akbar and Alexa.

In the next ten seconds, the heads of two other cops in the line exploded in a similar way. Absent was the sound of the rifle that fired those shots. Many in the crowd were unaware that anything had happened. Bud knew a sniper was doing this, but he couldn't tell where the bullets came from.

As the crowd sensed something amiss, the throng of marchers bulged outwards, trying to get away, but most were hemmed in by the mob of Klansmen surging forward. The speakers on the podium crouched down and tried to get down the short set of steps so they too could get away.

The mob surged forward. Bud saw Jimmy Ray shed his Klan robe when he was about fifty feet from the podium.

Bud tried to push through the crowd separating him from Alexa. He had ceased to be a policeman at that point and was concentrating only on saving the woman he loved.

More ax handles appeared, and the Klan began to beat the black marchers. The crowd of blacks surged toward him, and Bud was pushed away from the podium—away from Roscoe, away from Abkar, and worst of all, away from Alexa.

He tried to push through the crowd but could make no headway against the fear-driven people. Keeping his eye on Alexa, he spoke into his radio.

"The shit's hitting the fan. We need the National Guard out here now!"

He tried to catch Alexa's eye and motion her away from the Klan. The group still on the podium seemed paralyzed with indecision or disbelief.

Jimmy Ray used his ax handle to part the crowd. Bud watched him grab both Akbar and Alexa by the arm and hustle them away from the mob of Klansmen. They seemed to go with Jimmy Ray willingly.

Bud watched as Jimmy Ray pulled them both across MLK toward Piedmont Avenue. When they were halfway across the street, a rusted-out white Plymouth backed up Piedmont, going the wrong way. The car stopped and waited as Jimmy Ray pushed both Akbar and Alexa into the backseat.

Bud strained to see the driver and the license plate. The plate would have been visible except for the thick layer of red dirt that covered it.

Before the Plymouth sped away north on Piedmont, Bud noticed the driver's long blond ponytail.

PART III

I been searchin' my soul tonight
Don't wanna be alone in life
Now I know I can shine a light
To find my way back home
—Vonda Shepherd

Chapter 24

Away!

Saturday, October 28

"Who the hell are you?" spat out Alexa as the car spun around and sped north on Piedmont with squealing tires.

The man with the ponytail was driving and turned around to wink at her.

He was the one at the strip club on Fulton Industrial, Alexa thought. *He might have driven that dump truck.*

"We're just a coupla guys worried 'bout you in that mob," Ponytail said after a moment as he regarded her in the rearview mirror.

"So what about Congressman Lewis, the rest of them?" asked Akbar.

"You an' the lady was in the newspaper," he said.

"Stop the car and let us out right now," said Akbar with an imperious ring of command in his voice.

"Unh-unh," Ponytail told him. "We innerested in the two o' you. By the way, you can call me Face, an' this here's Jimmy Ray."

Jimmy Ray jabbed him as he said it. The Plymouth swerved, and Alexa shared a look of consternation with Akbar.

"What the fuck, Jimmy Ray," said Face, "you tell 'em."

"Yeah, but what about? Waters?" said Jimmy Ray.

"What about him?" said Face as he braked for the light at North Avenue.

"He told us what to do."

"We'll do most of it." He gestured with his head at Alexa. "Hey, check her out. I wanna get there, have a little fun 'fore Waters comes."

Alexa was sitting behind the driver. Akbar lunged across her and snaked a strong brown arm around Ponytail's throat.

"You stop the car now!" he commanded the driver through clenched teeth.

The Plymouth swerved across two lanes as Face fought to keep control.

A gun appeared in Jimmy Ray's hand. Akbar was twisting the driver's thick blond hair when he noticed the small, deadly black circle pointed at his right eye.

"Take your hands off him," Jimmy Ray said, "and sit back. Otherwise, both you and the lady get it."

Akbar hesitated.

"Now," said Jimmy Ray and shot a hole in the roof of the car.

Stunned, Akbar released the man and slumped in his seat, sharing another look with Alexa—this time a look of despair.

When Bud saw the Plymouth drive off, he radioed for pursuit. Another agent snaked a g-car through the crowd that was scattering across Martin Luther King Drive after the assault by the Klan. Bud jumped in.

"I'm Bud Prior, hate crimes. Head north on Piedmont."

The driver flipped on the siren and took off north. Piedmont was deserted all the way up to Tenth Street.

"Where could they have gone?" fretted Bud.

"Were me," said the other agent, "I'd have gotten on that interstate, the downtown connector at Baker Street. They could be anywhere."

Bud was deeply worried about Alexa. When he thought about what one of them would do to a beautiful woman like Alexa, he imagined the worst.

Bud prayed; it was all that was left for him.

"Put out an APB on the Plymouth," said Bud, "and then let's go back to the capitol. I wanna talk to Roscoe. Hopefully, the National Guard'll be there now."

Back at the capitol, Bud found Roscoe nursing a deep gash on his head and sitting on the low wall that separated the capitol grounds from the sidewalk.

"Fuckers got me," Roscoe said. "National Guard got here just after you left. A lot of the Kluckers are in custody across the street. We've been running anyone injured over to Grady Hospital in APD units."

Roscoe looked tired and defeated.

"You okay, Roscoe?"

"Need to get my head looked at. Guy clipped me good with an ax handle. Hey, I saw they got Alexa and Akbar. We need to find them both soon. They're the most visible people here—famous now—after the newspaper, after their speeches. Now they're kidnapped."

Bud felt an intense wave of guilt wash over him and hung his head.

"Bud," said Roscoe, "nothing anyone could do. This march was gonna happen. We'll find 'em."

"Roscoe, it's late and I've got to get home to get a sitter to stay with Christopher for the night. Call me from the hospital."

Alexa was thrown against Akbar as the driver of the Plymouth hung a right just before the Georgia Power Building, climbed the hill on Highland Avenue, and took the long curving on-ramp to the connector. Jimmy Ray breathed a huge sigh of relief when they merged into the interstate traffic.

The driver kept the Plymouth at a steady sixty-five and took I-75 north toward Marietta. He got off on Delk Road heading west, went past the Lockheed plant, under the railroad overpass, and took a left on Atlanta Road.

Alexa stared bleakly out the window at the obvious poverty of Atlanta Road. Rickety mobile homes lined the red dirt driveways of the trailer parks on the west side of the road. Seedy massage parlors, pawn shops, and an occasional convenience store with barred windows lined the east side.

The driver took a right into Jonquil Trailer Park and bounced down the rough driveway. There were no lights, and the ruts couldn't be seen in the darkness. Alexa and Akbar bumped their heads on the roof of the car when the Plymouth bottomed out in one of the deeper ruts.

Alexa wondered how she could possibly get a message to Bud.

The blond-haired man called Face parked the Plymouth next to a tiny mobile home with a rickety porch.

"Jimmy Ray, cover them while I go inside," Face commanded.

"I don't have to show you the gun again, do I?" said Jimmy Ray.

Alexa shared another bleak look with Akbar. The man called Face entered the trailer and came out a few minutes later. He gestured with his head for them to get out of the car.

Inside the mobile home, the living room floor was covered with a dirty green carpet. The only furniture was a stained blue couch and a color television.

A diminutive, dark-haired woman lay on the couch, wearing cut-off jeans and a halter top. An open bag of corn chips lay on the floor in front of her.

"What is this shit?" she said.

"Take it easy, Tina," said Face. "Didn't Waters say we was comin'?"

"He don't tell me jack shit," she said with a Spanish accent.

"She a Meskin?" asked Jimmy Ray. "How come Waters knows a Meskin?"

"I'm a dancer," said Tina, standing up and showing off her well-shaped body.

"Ain't I seen you at Mama Gloria's?" asked Jimmy Ray.

"I dance there some," said Tina, smiling at him. "You like me?"

"Jimmy Ray, forget about her," said Face. "You need to be watchin' these two. Take 'em in the bedroom." He pointed to the other end of the mobile home. "There's some rope in there. Tie 'em both up an' take their shoes. They ain't goin' no place without shoes."

"I can't do it alone," protested Jimmy Ray.

"Tina, don't you fuckin' move," snarled Face.

In the bedroom, Face held the gun on Alexa while Jimmy Ray tied Akbar's hands behind his back.

"Tie his ankles too," said Face. "Then his wrists. Gag him too. Use this." Face pulled two dirty bandannas from his pocket. "One for each of 'em."

Face walked out of the bedroom. When Alexa felt Jimmy Ray behind her with his hands on her wrists about to tie her hands together, she pulled away and clawed at his crotch, until she found his testicles through his pants. She squeezed and yanked. Jimmy Ray screamed and fell writhing to the floor.

Alexa turned toward Akbar and began to untie him. She heard movement and looked up to see Face's hand coming at her. God, that hurt, she thought, as the blow to her cheek and ear knocked her away from Akbar. Her knees felt weak and she fell to the floor.

Jimmy Ray still lay on the floor, moaning and holding his crotch.

"Jimmy Ray, I swear!" yelled Face. "Do I have to do everything?"

Her head still fuzzy, Alexa felt Face pick her up roughly under the arms and throw her on the bed. He tied each of her wrists and ankles to the bedframe, spread-eagling her on the thin grimy sheet.

When Face was done tying Alexa, he leaned over and gave her a lascivious grin. He touched her face as he leaned toward her. Alexa spat in his eye.

"Bitch, don't you ever learn?" he said, as he gagged her with the other bandanna.

He helped Jimmy Ray get up and led him out of the bedroom.

"Better get your shit together, Jimmy Ray," Alexa heard him say. "Claude'll be here soon."

Alexa felt incredibly vulnerable spread-eagled on the bed. She craned her neck and could just see the top of Akbar's head. She looked around the room, trying to think of a way out.

Then Face walked slowly into the bedroom, a nasty grin distorting his mouth. He threw a towel from the bathroom over Akbar's head.

"I don't want us givin' him a show," he told Alexa.

Alexa knew what was coming and twisted against her bonds.

Face reached down and caressed her cheek. Then he reached down and, in a sudden movement, ripped away her blouse and thin lace bra.

Alexa heard the sharp sound of his inhalation when he saw her nakedness.

She closed her eyes and steeled her nerves for what was about to come.

Her panicky thoughts tumbled over each other. *Is this going to hurt? Will he kill me when it's done?* She felt his fingers fumbling with her skirt and panty hose.

Then Alexa heard a sharp meaty crack, the sound of a fist hitting bone. She opened her eyes and saw the skinhead from the foundry standing at the foot of the bed, a snarl on his lips.

"What the fuck you think you were doin', Face? Keepin' your dick happy ain't what this is about. You guys are so clueless."

"C'mon, Claude," Face whined. "What the hell difference does it make? You ain't plannin' to give her back, are ya?"

"You don't know what my plans are."

Alexa saw the skinhead kick hard at where she figured Face was lying on the floor. She heard a grunt as the skinhead's foot landed.

"I explained to you that both of them are political prisoners. We're using them to changes people's thinking, people's ideology."

Face stood up. A bruise was darkening his left cheek.

"It don't make no difference, Waters. You got no right to treat me like this."

"Fuck you, Face. This is gonna be done right."

Face stared hard at the other man. His ponytail had come undone, and his long blond hair hung in his face. Behind the hair was a look of fear and hatred.

"Fuck you too, Claude," Faced growled at him, then hawked up a loogie from deep in his throat and spat in the skinhead's face.

The skinhead reared back, cocked his arm, and landed a wild haymaker right on Face's jaw. The force of the blow propelled him backward, and he crashed into the window. The sharp edge of a broken pane cut into his neck. Bright red arterial blood jetted from the cut, and Face collapsed to the floor.

Alexa could see Face's head tilted forward at an odd angle. The blood continued to flow as he lay unmoving.

"Miss Mason," the skinhead said as he untied her wrists. He looked her straight in the eyes, and she could see he was consciously keeping himself from staring at her breasts. "I am truly sorry this little incident happened. I made it clear you were to be restrained but otherwise treated with respect. I'll get you some clothes."

He rummaged in the closet and came out with a pair of black balloon pants with elastic cuffs, the kind that body builders wear, and a Mickey Mouse T-shirt.

He dropped the clothes on top of Alexa and leaned over to untie her ankles. Alexa could smell him, a mixture of gun oil and sweat. The rough masculine smell was strangely comforting.

"Akbar. Uncover him please," she said as she removed her gag herself.

Claude pulled the towel from the supine Akbar's head.

As Alexa dressed, Claude untied Akbar. She felt both sets of eyes on her body, and she hurried to cover up. The T-shirt was too tight, and she was painfully conscious that, with no bra, she looked too provocative.

"Please," she asked, "could I look for some other clothes?"

"Certainly," said Claude. "As I said, both of you should have been treated with respect. You are here to help spread my ideology. Personally, I bear you no ill will."

"Then why have you done this?" Akbar entreated. "Why won't you let us go?"

"Muhammad, you want the children to be your messengers, right?"

Akbar nodded.

"Well, you and the lady are going to be my messengers."

"So what's your message?" said Alexa, coming out of the closet. She had found a darker T-shirt that was not so revealing, and she wore a black windbreaker of shiny material that seemed to go with the pants.

A long moment went by. Claude looked at Akbar first, then at Alexa, his face blank.

"I'm going to have to keep you tied up. I need you, but it's not part of my plan to do you harm."

"But what do you want? What are these plans you have for us?" Akbar persisted.

"I'll let you know," Claude told them. "Please come with me now. I can't leave you alone."

Alexa followed Claude out to the living room. Akbar walked slowly behind her.

Jimmy Ray still sat on the couch next to Tina.

"Get outta here, Jimmy Ray," said Claude. "You too, Tina. You can come back later. Tina, don't forget what I told you."

"Where am I gonna go, Claude?" Jimmy Ray hissed at the skinhead.

"You think I give a shit?"

Jimmy Ray stood up and walked out the door with Tina following.

The skinhead pulled the gun from his pants and held it loosely against his hip.

"Like I said, I'm going to treat you with consideration and respect, but I can't let you leave." He deliberately positioned himself between them and the door.

"Who are you?" Alexa asked. "I saw you at Seitzman's Foundry."

"My name is Claude Waters. As far as I can tell, I'm the one who's going to change the direction this country is going. We are not going to have a black man in the White House ever again. I put the dirt in the playgrounds, and that's only the start."

"What?" exclaimed Akbar and Alexa together.

Akbar stared at the man in horror and disbelief.

"You . . . you monster," Alexa hissed at him after a moment of stunned silence. "How could you do something so evil?"

Chapter 25

Not So Simple to Escape

Sunday, October 29

Alexa woke at dawn. She stood up and stretched with her eyes shut. She looked around the small trailer. Waters still sat on the floor. He yawned once and grinned at her.

"What are you going to do with us?" she asked, exasperation in her voice. "You've kept us overnight. Isn't that enough to make whatever point it is you have?"

"I need you to get on board with my message," answered Claude. "You and the nigger are gonna be the ones to tell it to the world. Who better?"

"Not me," she said, glaring at him.

Akbar awoke. He rolled his head on his neck. Alexa could hear his joints creak.

"You awake now, monkey boy?" asked Claude.

Akbar sniffed and looked hard at the man.

"You wanna know why I'm doing this?" said Claude. "A nigger killed my parents, orphaned me when I was eight years old. My mother was pregnant, and my father was taking her to the hospital. They got hit by a logging truck just as they pulled out of the driveway. At least they didn't suffer. Nigger was driving the truck. A thing like that's hard to forget.

"Another thing. Having niggers live here in this country has damaged the white race. Made a lot of us soft. We shouldn't have used slaves in the first place way back when. Should have left the niggers in Africa where they belong. Thing is, what are we gonna do about it now?"

"You are crazy, man, to blame your racism and hatred on slavery," said Akbar. "If you weren't evil enough to mean it, I would laugh. What is it you really want?"

Waters stood and massaged his lower back.

"Ms. Mason asked me that yesterday. Well, the two of you are gonna be my messengers. I'm still thinkin' on exactly what I want you to say."

"Waters, I don't know why you feel you can blame my entire race for what one man did to you. It is hard to lose your parents. It would be especially hard to lose them at eight years old. But your thinking isn't rational."

"Oh, yeah," challenged Claude. His back was up. "If I'm so irrational, how come all those Klan guys at the rally feel the same way? White Christian men and niggers can't live together in the same country." Drops of spit sprayed from his mouth as he yelled.

Alexa put a hand on Akbar's arm. She was afraid and she wanted him to stop provoking the skinhead. She remembered Waters flying off the handle and killing Face.

Waters muttered at them and walked out of the trailer.

"We've got to find a way out of here, Akbar," she whispered. "The guy is dangerous. He's not in control of himself and he's an ideologue. Don't provoke him again. He killed that guy in the bedroom in a fit of anger."

"Alexa, he's got to sleep sometime."

"Does he?" asked Alexa. "Do we know whether he slept last night? I'll bet he didn't."

"So some time he'll get sleepy," said Akbar. "He's also got to deal with the dead guy in the bedroom. He needs the other guy, Jimmy Ray."

"Waters flew off the handle at Jimmy Ray too, Akbar. Kicked him out. I don't know if Jimmy Ray'll be back. You heard it; you were there too. That's what I'm worried about. He can't control his rage." She shuddered in fear and hugged herself before continuing. "Claude is not in control of himself even though he believes his intentions are good."

"You're right." Akbar nodded. "We have to keep our mouths shut."

Akbar walked over to the window opposite the couch. A portion of the driveway that led out of the trailer park was visible.

"If we could make it to the road," he mused, "we'd probably be okay."

"I don't know, Akbar. There's what—about a hundred yards to the road? A long way barefoot. Plenty of time for him to see us."

"We'll do it when it gets dark. We can wait."

They stayed on the couch and dozed for another hour. When they both woke up again at about eight o'clock that morning, Waters was sitting between them and the door, his back propped against the wall and a thousand-yard stare.

Jimmy Ray snored on the floor nearby. There was no sign of the woman.

"Look, I'm sure you two talked about escaping while I was gone," said Waters when he saw they were awake. "Don't even think about it. I can stay awake as long as I need to." His easy smile sent chills down Alexa's spine. "I'm one of those guys that don't need much sleep. Besides, any time I get a little tired, I got Jimmy Ray to take over for an hour or so."

Waters got up and went into the kitchen. He rustled around for a few minutes until the odors of cooking permeated the tiny trailer.

"Breakfast," he said, carrying plates of scrambled eggs and toast to the kitchen table. "Wake up, Jimmy Ray. Time to eat."

Akbar convinced Alexa she needed to eat to keep her strength up. She gave in, and realizing she was hungry, wolfed the plate of eggs and toast.

"You clean up," said Waters to Alexa when everyone had finished. Akbar helped her clear the table and wash the dishes.

Waters and Jimmy Ray disappeared into the bedroom and came out carrying Face's body by his wrists and ankles. They carried the body outside, leaving their two captives alone.

Through the mobile home window, Alexa and Akbar watched the two men load the body in a white Ford van. Jimmy Ray got in and drove off.

Claude came back inside. "I can't have you trying to escape," he said. "I'm going to have to tie you up again."

Chapter 26

Some Steel

Sunday, October 29

When Bud had gotten home late after the rally the night before, he had paid the sitter double for having to stay late. Earlier, he had considered asking the sitter to stay the night so he could go back out to look for Alexa but decided that Christopher needed some sense of normalcy.

When the sitter left, Bud had crept into his son's room and watched his beautiful boy sleeping. His thoughts strayed to Alexa, to the enormity and likely futility of the task of finding her alive. He began to despair—for his own broken heart and for the impossibility of finding a woman with whom to share the life he had built for himself and his son.

The boy had flung one arm above his head. Bud could hear the breath in his throat. He began to weep silently as he stood there watching his son sleep.

Bud continued weeping as he went back to bed. As he lay there, nursing his broken heart, he felt some steel, a resolve inside himself. *She's not dead yet*, he told himself. *You can find her!*

Bud knew that if he couldn't get her back, something rare and precious inside him—perhaps his ability to love anyone—would be lost forever.

That resolve enabled him to get a few hours of fitful sleep, knowing he would need as much rest as he could get for whatever happened next.

A Toxic Assault

Bud mixed up some batter and fed Christopher his favorite breakfast—pancakes.

"Christopher, I have to go into work today. Here's what's happened. Many, many black children have been hurt—poisoned—on purpose. It's a really terrible thing. You remember our conversation about treating everybody well whatever color their skin is?"

"Sure, Dad."

"Alexa was there and . . . and she was kidnapped by some people, maybe the same ones who poisoned the children. I'm so worried about her, Christopher, and I've got to try and save her."

Bud could see a great sob building in his son's chest and held him as the boy cried.

"I'm scared, Dad. Alexa's great. Please save her."

"I'm gonna try, Christopher."

"It's hard to remember Mom. It seems like a long time ago."

"Son, I've always been afraid about what you've missed." Bud held Christopher tightly. "I love you so much, son. I wanted To protect you from getting hurt. I didn't know how much you missed Sandi . . . your mother, and I was afraid to ask."

Bud had a brief thought that what he was saying, trying to communicate, was too advanced for an eight-year-old. *It doesn't matter,* he told himself. *Christopher's got to hear this.*

"Son, I lost your mother and couldn't bear the thought of losing someone else. If I didn't get involved, I couldn't get hurt. That's why I haven't found anyone else. Do you understand?"

The boy nodded.

"I have to go into the office, and you'll have to come with me. There's no time to find a sitter. Can you bring a coloring book, something to do?"

At his office, Bud logged onto the NCIC, the National Crime Information Computer, and searched for individuals involved in hate crimes in the southeast. After going through about a hundred mug shots, there was no one who even closely resembled the ponytailed driver.

Bud sighed in frustration. He looked over at Christopher and saw that the boy was engrossed in *The Little Engine that Could.*

I think I can, I think I can! Bud found new determination in the familiar childhood mantra and started a new search, this time for assault and battery arrests in Atlanta within the last year. His reasoning—that someone involved in the kidnapping might have a short fuse.

He found six men with ponytails but only one blond man. The guy's given name was Segovia Lavoris Chism. *What the hell kind of a name is that?* he wondered.

The address given was in a poor neighborhood between Glen Iris and Boulevard near the Atlanta police station in City Hall East.

Staring at the mug shot on the computer screen, Bud had a strong hunch that this was the man who drove the Plymouth.

It's time to move on this, he thought

The location of the address was on the way home. Bud called and arranged for a sitter at home. Then he printed out two copies of the mug shot and walked to his car with Christopher.

"I've got to make a stop on the way home. It's important."

"That's fine, Dad."

Bud found the address. It was a small ramshackle house on Rankin Street, five houses up from a tiny church on the corner of Glen Iris. Bud found a parking place right in front. He couldn't help notice the two hookers sitting and smoking on the low wall that separated the church lawn from the sidewalk. The blonde one waved, hoping he was a trick.

"Christopher, I'm going to lock you in the car. Don't let anyone in."

He got out, locked the car, and then went up to the house and knocked on the front door.

"Just a minute," came a woman's voice from inside. There was the sound of someone moving around inside the house, and then the door opened on the chain.

"Yes," said a woman peering out beneath the chain. Her blue eyes were narrowed against the smoke from the cigarette in her hand, and Bud could see part of a riot of blonde curls.

"I'm Agent Prior of the FBI." He held up his shield and put it away quickly. "I was wondering if you've ever seen this man?" He held up one of the mug shots.

"Mister, I don't talk to cops, not if I don't have to."

"I understand. Please, this would be strictly off the record."

"Look," she said, "I've had a bunch of trouble with cops before. I don't want that again. You got some money?"

Bud sniffed and looked down a moment. He quickly but quietly stuck his foot into the gap between the door and the frame.

"You don't have to even come out. Talk to me through the doorway like this. I really need to know who this guy is."

"How much?" she said.

Bud looked in his wallet. "I've got forty bucks on me. That's the best I can do."

"I don't have to come outside."

"Nope—and I don't have to come in."

"Okay. I'm gonna unhook the door."

The door closed a moment and opened again. Bud was confronted with a petite blonde woman. She was slender and pretty and had remarkably large firm breasts beneath the dark green tank top she wore. The cut-off jeans showed off tanned, shapely legs.

"You understand why I don't like cops?"

"You're a . . . working girl."

"You got it. I'm trying to pay off these tits. That's why I'm staying here in such a dump."

"I won't take much of your time." Bud pulled out the mug shot and showed it to her again.

"Forty bucks?"

He pulled the money from his wallet and held it up.

"His name. Then I'll give it to you."

"His street name is Face." She snatched the money from his hand as she said it. "He's got some fucked up name his momma done give him. He's a good lookin' dude. That's why they call him Face."

"When did you last see him?"

"'Bout three, four days ago, middle of the week. Guy's in and out. Not since then."

Bud was suspicious. "You don't like him, do you?" he asked.

"You talk to the Atlanta cops?" Her hand was on the door about to close it.

"Not about you. That's a promise. I don't even know your name, and I don't want to know."

"Fine, Mr. FBI. Face brought me a customer coupla weeks ago—a no pay. I ain't strong—you can see that—an' I refuse to split my take with anyone. That's why I gotta get outta here and find a place in Buckhead, somewhere upscale.

"Thing is, with Face around, he's my enforcer and I don't have to fuck with someone's hand in the till. I give him an occasional freebie. It's worth it. Know what I'm saying?"

Bud nodded. "So Face comes and goes from here? You know him from anywhere else?"

"Nope. We just split the rent, sometimes with a coupla other folks. Cheaper that way. I got my own room. Upstairs. Private. I still don't use it much, mostly do outcall."

She took a drag from her cigarette and looked at him hard for a moment.

"But what the fuck am I tellin' you all this for? I think you already got your money's worth."

The door slammed, and Bud was left staring at its peeling paint.

Chapter 27

A Prophet No More

Monday morning, October 30

Alexa woke, curled up on the dirty sofa in the living room of the mobile home. The bathroom light was on, and its thin fluorescent glow crept along the length of the trailer, turning the darkness of the living room to a gloom that matched her mood of despair.

Gradually her eyes adjusted to the dimness, and Alexa could see Akbar sleeping a few feet away from her. She wiggled her hands inside the rope that held them. By squeezing her left thumb toward her palm, she was able to make her hand small enough to slip out of the bonds. When her hands were free, she untied her feet. She checked her watch—three minutes until 4:00 a.m. Everyone would be asleep.

Alexa looked around the room. Waters was gone. Jimmy Ray sat on the floor leaning against the wall. Alexa couldn't tell if he was asleep or not—until he began to snore.

She crept over to Akbar and woke him, placing a hand on his mouth so he wouldn't speak. She pointed to Jimmy Ray, pantomimed sleep, and pointed at the door. Then she untied him.

The opportunity was not lost on Akbar. They tiptoed past the sleeping man. Alexa gently pushed open the door, and then they were outside the trailer, trying to get their bearings in the darkness.

Akbar pointed to the right and took her hand. He led her along the red dirt driveway. Their bare feet made progress painfully slow.

Akbar was still holding her hand when they reached Atlanta Road. No traffic cruised by. They crossed and headed away from their captors toward a strip mall across the street.

The pair had not gone very far when they heard tires spinning on gravel and then squealing on asphalt.

They were in front of the strip mall and could see no way to get behind the row of low buildings where they could hide.

The sound of an engine and squealing tires approached from behind. The van pulled up in front of them. Waters pointed his gun out the window.

"Not so fast," he said. "Jimmy Ray shouldn't have been asleep, but now you're gonna get in the van and come back." He held up the gun prominently. "I'd say you got no choice. Don't think I won't kill you."

Crestfallen, they got back in the van.

Back at the trailer, Waters gestured at them with the gun, indicating they should get out of the van and back in the trailer.

Once inside, Waters turned on all the lights, and the three of them sat and stared at each other until well past daybreak.

"Muhammad," Waters began, "I don't know why you and I can't give a common message. What we believe is not that different."

"How can you say that?" Akbar burst out. "You are a man full of hate. I can't understand how anyone could possibly harm children the way you have."

"Maybe our methods are different," said Waters, "but our goals are essentially the same. You feel as I do that the racial divide within this country is unacceptable and something must be done."

Alexa stared at both men with interest as Akbar nodded for Waters to continue.

"It was a base impulse," Waters began, "that first made white men take slaves. It was laziness. It is that same impulse we see today permeating our entire culture. Why is it we have the highest rate of, what is it, attention deficit disorder? I'll tell you. As a nation, a culture, we're too lazy to pay attention long enough for any more than a quick shallow impression. TV and the rest of the media just make it worse."

"So why do you blame this on people of color?" asked Akbar. "The base impulse you're speaking of is part of all of us, white or black."

"No." Waters was adamant. "We were infected . . . corrupted by the slaves brought over here."

"You are wrong." Akbar was equally vehement. "You know Thomas Pynchon? In *Gravity's Rainbow*, he wrote that the colonies were a place where a lily-white European could relax and enjoy the smell of his own shit. This perception is the true sin of racism—seeing the other as lesser than oneself. The Europeans made colonies in Africa long before the United States existed. But the base impulse did not begin with European colonialists who saw a chance to exploit and subjugate a less technically developed people. Centuries before, in Africa and the Middle East, slavery was an institution. The Book of Exodus in the Old Testament is about escaping slavery. The base impulse you speak of is a human impulse. No one was corrupted—the evil is present in all men! It is up to each of us to recognize this evil and to overcome it."

"You're fucked up, man." Waters was angry now. "You went to college. I read that article 'bout you in the paper. Is this the shit they taught you at that nigger college? You wouldn't have even had a college to go to if it wasn't for white men!"

Akbar was silent.

"You ain't talkin' now," Waters taunted Akbar. "You know I'm right. You just refuse to admit it like all the other niggers. So how did you get to be a leader? You sure ain't smart enough."

Akbar stared at Waters for a full minute before he spoke.

"What you don't realize is that knowledge without morality is evil. I don't know how you propose to change this country. You seem to have no ideology, no message. You say you are high and noble. You did save this woman from that animal. It was the right thing to do, but you are not noble. Would you have saved her if she were black? You are not using us to make an ideological point to the world. Instead, you've kidnapped us just to get your fifteen minutes of fame."

Claude stared at Akbar. His eyes grew red and angry as he listened to the black man's indictment.

"We've been with you," Akbar continued, "for four days now, and from an intellectual and ideological viewpoint, I still have no idea what it is you want. You say you want me to join you in a call for segregation. Even if I believed that segregation was an answer to America's problems with race, I could not support you. You've given me no position, no consistent set of beliefs from which you reason. I can't and I won't support you."

Alexa was sitting next to Akbar on the couch and nudged him with her toe to make him stop baiting Waters.

Claude walked up to Akbar and spat words in his face in a hot angry whisper. "You're not gonna do this. I gotta keep you in one piece, but that doesn't mean I can't use the girl here to leverage you."

"Waters, will you be able to trust me? You'll always be wondering what I'll say," retorted Akbar. "You can threaten Ms. Mason, and I'll do what you say as far as being somewhere at a certain time. Of course, I'll still be your prisoner. You've got a gun, but you'll never be able to control my mind, and you'll never know whether what I said helped you or doomed you to hell where you belong. See, one advantage of that 'nigger' college is that I'm able to choose my words."

Akbar gave their captor a small hostile smile. Alexa looked at Claude; his face was bright red with anger. She put her hand across Akbar's mouth to get him to stop. He looked at her in surprise and removed her hand.

"You know, Waters," continued Akbar, "I don't think you have any real agenda. I think you're just a thug. Maybe you were starved for love when you were a kid and that's the source of all this anger. I don't—"

Claude pulled the gun from the waistband of his jeans and shot Akbar in the chest.

Alexa screamed.

"You shut up now or I'll shut you up too," Waters hissed her, his voice edgy.

Alexa kneeled next to Akbar on the dirty carpet. She held his head. He looked up at her and smiled. He turned his head away from her, and a dark torrent of blood flowed from his mouth.

"The races should be together," Akbar said in a hoarse whisper. "We learn from each other, black and white. Tell them, tell . . ."

He stopped speaking and smiled again with a faraway light in his eyes.

"Stay with me, Akbar," she pleaded as tears rolled down her cheeks.

He looked at her again and started to speak. "I . . ."

Then the light went out of his eyes for good.

Alexa let out a sob and a wail.

"Why did you kill him?" she screamed at Waters.

"Shut up!" commanded Waters. "I have to think and I can't be listenin' to you cryin'!"

He pulled her roughly away from Akbar.

"We gotta get outta here," he said and led her out to the van.

Chapter 28

The Pickle Factory

Monday, October 30

In spite of the kidnapping, for Christopher's sake, Bud did not abandon the daily routine. Monday morning after taking his son to school, Bud was sitting at his desk at the FBI offices staring at the phone. The kidnapping had made the newspapers. There were five FBI agents put on the case and at least ten APD detectives. No one really knew where to look.

Roscoe had left a message on his voice mail saying he wouldn't be in for a couple of days. Saturday night, he had been diagnosed with a moderate concussion, and the doctors had told him to stay home.

At four minutes till ten, the phone rang.

"Agent Prior, this is Doctor Reston at the state crime lab. You wanted some DNA testing on that cloth you brought in."

"Yes," said Bud, worried about Alexa and not that interested in the blood on Jimmy Ray's Klan robe for the moment.

"It was blood on that piece of cloth. We had a hell of a time doing the DNA, but finally we got it. Had to do a serial PCR."

"Whatever," said Bud. "Did it match that tissue sample I left there?"

"Sure did. I'll put the report in the mail."

The coroner had given Jack Williams's cause of death as blood loss after having his throat cut.

"Thank you, Doctor Reston."

Bud hung up the phone and then started to dial the number at Jimmy Ray's mobile home, hoping to talk to Melanie Groover. He stopped half way through, not wanting to connect with Jimmy Ray on the phone and tip him off.

I suppose I could drive out there, he thought. *There's still time today, and there are no other leads on where Alexa might be.*

Although it had been sunny in Atlanta when he left, a light drizzle fell from a gray sky when Bud pulled his truck up to the Groover mobile home at 11:30 a.m.

Melanie Groover answered his knock almost immediately. Her eyes were red-rimmed, and her cheeks were wet.

"Come in, please, Agent Prior." She indicated he should sit at the kitchen table. She stared at the floor a moment before sitting at the table across from him.

"Jimmy Ray was here yesterday, but I ain't seen him since. He showed up driving a beat-up white van that I ain't seen before."

"He was at the Klan rally, Ms. Groover, and the suspicions you shared with me on Friday were correct. I think he was up to his ears in this Klan thing."

Melanie shrugged, a small moue of displeasure and regret turning down the corners of her mouth. Bud figured she was all cried out.

"You have no idea where Jimmy Ray is now, do you, Ms. Groover?"

"No, an' I don't actually plan on seeing him again. I talked about it with my mama. She helped me figure out Jimmy Ray ain't the one for me. She helped me see that. She told me I would have to be strong and that it would be better to be single than have my girls exposed to all that hate stuff. She helped me find a part-time job, and I'm just about makin' ends meet."

"You've been busy," said Bud.

"Well, sir," she told him, "my mama never liked Jimmy Ray, and she figured this day would come. She had a job set up for me already.

"Anyway, when Jimmy Ray came home, I asked him why he lied to me about being in the Klan. I told him I saw you pull that Klan robe from under the trailer. He told me all he did was go to a few meetings. I could tell he was lying. He told me—get a load of this—that what he was doing with the Klan was important for America and that he'd been working with a man he met at the foundry. He said the man had a message that would solve the race problem in America. Jimmy Ray said the man was talking to that Muhammad fella, the guy who led the march. You know, it was in the paper."

Bud nodded.

"So I called him on it, Sergeant Prior. I asked him flat out if he was involved in poisoning those children and in the kidnappings, the Muhammad fella and that lady. I told him if he was involved that I was done with him. I told him I'd make sure he'd never see the girls again. He told me it wasn't a kidnapping. I told him the papers and the TV said it was a kidnapping.

"Then he didn't say anything for about a minute. I could tell he was thinkin' hard about what I said. Then he told me the Muhammad fella was at one of those trailer parks in Marietta. I think he said Atlanta Road."

Why would Jimmy Ray share that piece of information? Bud wondered. *This seems almost too easy. Is it a setup?*

"I told Jimmy Ray he had to turn himself in. He's a criminal and I won't have him around my girls. I told him that I would always love him but it wasn't enough."

Melanie started to cry, but she continued. "I told him that he had to make things right and pay his dues to society. How could he be a father to these girls if we were all ashamed of him?"

"Did he say anything else, Ms. Groover?"

"No, sir. He just went to the tool shed, got a shovel, and drove away in that white van."

Bud turned onto Atlanta Road, saw signs for trailer parks stretching into the distance before him, and shook his head.

He pulled into the first trailer park, parked his truck under a tree, and then knocked on the door of every mobile home. Whenever his knock went unanswered, he walked around and looked in the windows.

After searching four of the low-rent trailer parks, Bud came to one named Jonquil Trailer Park. Near the woods in the back, the door of one especially seedy looking mobile home was open. A beat-up white van and a white Plymouth were parked outside. The Plymouth looked a lot like the car Alexa had been forced into at the capitol.

Bud took a deep breath.

"Police, open up," he said as he knocked on the door of the mobile home. The door swung open from his knock, and Bud walked in with his shield out for ID and his gun in his hand.

Inside, Jimmy Ray sat slumped on the couch next to a small, dark-haired woman. They both looked up but otherwise did not acknowledge Bud.

Nearby on the floor lay the body of Akbar Muhammad, his shirt soaked with blood.

Bud was terrified for Alexa. If the kidnappers could kill Akbar, wouldn't they also see Alexa as just a throw-away hostage? With his heart pounding, he donned a pair of latex gloves and examined Akbar's lifeless body. Could Alexa still be alive? He took another deep breath to calm himself.

"How did he die, Jimmy Ray?" asked Bud.

"Gunshot in the chest," said Jimmy Ray. "I wasn't here. I figger Waters did it."

"Claude Waters?" asked Bud. "The guy at the foundry?"

"That's him," said Jimmy Ray. "He hired me to work the backhoe."

"Does he have Alexa Mason?"

"Don't know, but she was here, so probably," answered Jimmy Ray. "Fucker kicked me outta here. After what I did for him!"

Bud drew his revolver.

"I'm arresting both of you. Suspicion of murder."

"Hey!" Jimmy Ray became belligerent. "Wasn't me! You need to find Waters."

As he held the gun on Jimmy Ray and the woman, Bud pulled out his phone and dialed Roscoe. Then he remembered that his partner wouldn't be at work. He canceled the call and instead dialed 911, identified himself as a police officer, and asked to be connected to the Cobb County Police Department.

"This is Sergeant Bud Prior of the APD. I'm on detail with the FBI and need some uniforms to take some suspects into custody," he told the officer who answered.

After giving his location, the officer assured him that a Cobb County unit and two officers would be there in less than ten minutes.

"Thanks," Bud told him and hung up.

The possibility of getting further leads from Jimmy Ray and this woman that might lead him to Alexa gave Bud hope.

"Tell me where they went," said Bud, his lips compressed in a thin tight line.

"I don't know where Waters is," pleaded Jimmy Ray. His tone was resigned. "I'd help you if I could. I know how bad this looks."

"You're still up to your neck in this," Bud told him. "The poisonings. You probably know about the body found out in the Cedartown landfill."

Jimmy Ray stared at him and gulped. "Look, I didn't kill this Muhammad guy. I didn't kill anybody. I wasn't even here when it happened. I got pissed off at Waters and left. Shit! I don't know what happened here."

"Who are you?" Bud asked the woman.

"I'm Tina Smith." Her Latin looks belied the name she gave.

"What'd you see?" Bud asked Tina.

"Nothin'. I was gone too," she said with a shrug.

Around the body of Akbar Muhammad, a thick puddle of dark blood had pooled on both sides of his chest. Bud could see the ragged entry wound through the hole in the dead man's shirt.

"Like you said, Groover. He's been shot. You're telling me you came in and found him and then did nothing?"

"That's right," said Jimmy Ray. "I knew Waters had done it. How else? I wasn't going to call the cops on him. I got nowhere else to go."

"You hear the shot?" Bud asked the woman.

"I didn't hear nothin'. I was at a friend's house down the road," said Tina.

"I was out in the woods in back for most of the night after Waters kicked me out," said Jimmy Ray. "I heard somethin' like a shot this mornin' 'bout nine. I didn't think nothin' of it at the time."

"So you don't know where Alexa Mason is?"

"I guess she's still with Waters," said Jimmy Ray. "Didn't see 'em leave."

Sirens sounded outside, and two uniformed Cobb County officers hurried into the mobile home.

"Thanks for coming so quick," said Bud. "I'm Sergeant Bud Prior of APD on detail to the FBI."

"Let us handcuff them for you, Sergeant," said one of the uniforms. Once the pair was in handcuffs and on their knees, the officer took their IDs.

"I can run these through the computer for you, Sergeant. We can connect from the unit."

"That be great, Officer Roberts," Bud told him, reading his name tag. "Can I come with you?"

"Joe, please watch 'em," Roberts said to his partner.

Bud and the officer shared first names as they walked to unit. The computer revealed that Jimmy Ray had no priors, whereas the woman, whose real name was Melinda Hernandez, had six previous arrests for prostitution and two for petty larceny.

"This is her listed address," said Roberts.

At least, that's some leverage, thought Bud.

Officer Roberts went back inside and helped his partner walk Jimmy Ray and Tina/Melinda to the unit. Bud stopped them as the officers were about to put them in the backseat.

"Look, Jimmy Ray" said Bud, "I can make things easier for you if you help me. I know you were at the march. I saw you kidnap both Akbar and Alexa. You're in a heap of trouble. I also know you were involved with Jack Wiliams's murder."

"I told you I can't help you. I just don't know! I'm losing everything. My wife said she never wants to see me again." His voice quavered, and Bud realized Jimmy Ray was at his emotional limit and likely didn't know anything about where Alexa or Waters might be.

"What about you?" Bud looked at Tina. "I know you got priors. You must know Waters. This is your place, and you let him hold hostages here. You'll be charged with aiding and abetting a kidnapping. Probably you'll do twenty years. So help yourself and take a guess where Waters would be."

Tina/Melinda stared at him a moment.

"Look, cop, I didn't do nothin'. Leave me outta this," she said. "I don't wanna go to jail." She started to cry. "I had nothing to do with the murder—or any of it. Let me go."

"Can't do that," said Bud, "but if you help me, I can let the DA know you were cooperative. Might help you later."

She sniffed and wiped her nose with the back of her hand.

"That fucking skinhead's been staying here on and off. He took me for a drive last week and showed me something. You know the old pickle factory downtown, near that MARTA station? He told me he knows how to sneak in there."

"Exactly where is it?"

"You know that parking lot that's closed by that MARTA station?"

"Yeah," said Bud, "on the south side of the King MARTA station."

"I dunno what the MARTA station's called, but it's near where those guys with the horse carriages go."

Bud knew exactly where it was. He nodded to the woman.

This still seems like it could be a setup, he thought. *I don't know how clever Waters is or what he had planned, but I've got to be extra careful.*

"I'm done," he told the uniforms and watched as they loaded Jimmy Ray and Tina/Melinda into the back of their unit.

"I'll make sure to let you know what to do with them soon."

"We got twenty-four hours, Sergeant Prior," said one the Cobb County men. "Take your time. It's clear you got other fish to fry."

"Thanks," said Bud as he ran for his truck.

Candler Pickles and Relish had been housed in a sturdy brick building on the corner of Martin Luther King and Grant Street near Oakland Cemetery. The business had declared bankruptcy in 1989, and the building had been vacant ever since.

An alley off Grant Street led to the old loading dock made of stone and timber. The loading dock area was fenced off with a chain link fence. A flap near the bottom had been cut and bent upward. Bud climbed through easily.

There was no door behind the loading dock. An archway led into a large dark room. His footsteps on the concrete floor echoed as Bud swept the beam of the flashlight around the cavernous room.

A metal staircase in a far corner led upstairs. On the second floor, a dark corridor stretched the length of the building. There was movement off to the left, and Bud heard a muffled cough.

Bud tried each door he came to. The first two were locked. When he opened the third one, he heard a groan.

He swung the light around the room. Alexa was lying on a dirty scrap of carpet in the corner.

This almost seems too easy, thought Bud. He moved into a dark corner behind the door.

Alexa's back was to him, and she moaned again. She was wearing a black satin jacket and black workout pants. On her feet were basketball high-tops several sizes too big for her.

After a few minutes, nothing had happened, and Bud couldn't stand just watching her tied up. He moved to her and unfastened her gag.

"Alexa. Thank God I found you! I've been so worried."

"Oh, Bud, it's a trap. You've got to be careful."

He turned around. No one else was in the room.

"I'll be back, Alexa," he said.

Bud went back into the corridor, his gun drawn, and searched the entire second floor of the building. He found no one else.

"There's no one here," said Bud as he bent to untie Alexa.

"Watch out!" he heard her scream as he worked the knot and felt something hard hit him on the side of the head. He blacked out.

When Bud came to, Alexa was gone. He felt shaky and nauseated, and his head hurt. He stood up on wobbly legs and hurried out of the pickle factory as fast as he could.

Outside, about a hundred yards away, he saw Waters holding Alexa's arm and pulling her into the shadows beneath the bridge holding up the MARTA tracks at the bottom of the hill. Bud ran after them.

King Memorial MARTA Station was at the bottom of the hill. Two long staircases provided passenger access to the elevated tracks. When he reached the staircase, Bud looked quickly around but couldn't see Alexa anywhere. He ran up the staircase to the platform but had to stop halfway, still dizzy.

The sound of the approaching train spurred him on. The doors were closing just as he got up to the platform. As the train began to move, he saw Alexa through a window. Her eyes beseeched him.

Waters held her arm loosely as they stood on the platform of the King Memorial station. The platform was otherwise deserted. A train pulled up in front of them, and Waters pushed Alexa onboard.

"That cop's pretty resourceful, ain't he? Findin' you like this," Waters said to Alexa when they were on the train. "He probably thinks he's really good. Don't realize how I set him up."

"He's tougher and smarter than you are. He'll find you, and if you hurt me . . ."

Alexa knew what a bad idea it was to provoke the man, but after seeing Bud, she couldn't help herself. "Waters, you know you've failed already. Akbar will be a martyr. You martyred him. In fact, you destroyed your own cause. You thought you were smarter than those other two, the ones who snatched me, but you're just another dumb cracker. He's going to find you, you know."

Alexa stared out the window as the train lurched and started to move. She saw Bud run along the platform toward the train, and the two stared at each other through the train windows.

Alexa looked over at Waters. He was looking forward toward the driver and had not seen Bud.

But the train was moving. What could Bud do?

Alexa prayed for the chance to know Bud as a friend and lover. She prayed for her own life and for Bud's courage and resourcefulness.

The train went by, gathering speed. There was nothing Bud could grab hold of on the smooth metal surface. Next to the door on the back of the last car were two metal handholds. Bud sprinted along the platform and launched himself at the rear door of the last car. He had to scramble on the coupling until his hands found the bars.

The train turned on the banked curve over the downtown connector toward Georgia State Station. Bud was flung to the right as the car banked. His left hand lost its grip, and he swung back and forth.

Inside the window, he could see a red lever labeled "Emergency Stop."

Bud smashed the window with his elbow and pulled the lever. The train lurched to a stop just inside the Georgia State Station.

Bud reached in through the broken glass and opened the back door. He ran through the train, his gun raised, frightening the passengers even more than the sudden stop.

At the front of the train, the driver was unconscious. A swatch of shiny black cloth was caught on the edge of the driver's open window.

Bud looked down the track. Waters was running along the tracks behind Alexa, holding a gun to her back.

Bud jackknifed out the window and began running along the track. He needed only seconds to find the rhythm so that his feet landed on every other crosstie. Electrical arcs jumped occasionally from the third rail to the ground, glowing blue even in the daylight.

Chapter 29

Reasons to Hate

Monday, October 30

The MARTA tracks passed through an open concrete gulch between the Georgia State and Five Points stations. As he ran, Bud watched Waters running along the track, pulling Alexa with him. When they hit the darkness on the other end of the gulch, they seemed to disappear.

Bud redoubled his efforts to catch up. Inside the dark tunnel, a set of tracks descended and turned away from him toward his left. To his right, a high chain link fence separated the MARTA tracks from the old railroad tracks that ran through downtown Atlanta. Neither Alexa nor Waters were in sight.

Bud heard the roar of an approaching MARTA train, and the headlight lit the track. As the train rounded the curve, Bud was blinded by the full glare of the headlights, but for an instant, he thought he saw two figures silhouetted against the approaching train. Then the train was almost upon him, and he jumped to the right and clung to the fence as the train roared by.

In the darkness after the headlights has passed, blue sparks jumped from the electrified third rail to the train.

Silently, Bud prayed for Alexa.

Alexa was being dragged along the tracks by Waters. He had given her a pair of size eleven basketball shoes that Face had left in the car, and she found running in them close to impossible.

"The train's coming," Claude told her as they heard the approaching screech of the wheels. "We'll jump off to the left. See where there's a roof over those other tracks, the ones turning left?" He pointed to the spur that allowed trains to connect between the north-south and east-west lines.

They were five yards away from the roof of the spur tunnel, and there was a fifteen-foot drop down to the spur itself.

"Hurry," urged Claude. They ran and jumped off the tracks, and two seconds later, the train went by.

"Look, Waters, I can't run in these shoes," wailed Alexa. "I'll only slow you down. Leave me. You can get away yourself."

"No way, Miss Mason, I'll wait for you. You still have a part in this, and I'll keep you with me. I'll tell you your part later 'cuz we're kinda busy right now," he hissed.

He pulled Alexa along another forty yards until they came to the service door on the platform of the Five Points Station. Claude craned his head around the corner, then slipped open the door and pushed Alexa through.

"Act normal," he whispered. "I can kill you before anyone reacts."

"But you won't. You need me somehow. You said so."

"Yes, I need you, but don't make me need to kill you worse than I need you, Miss Mason."

"I'll end up a martyr too. Like Akbar will be, like Martin Luther King. You'll never achieve what you want." Alexa knew she shouldn't provoke him but couldn't help herself—there was something absolutely maddening about his intransigence.

Claude stared at her for a moment.

"Look, just c'mon," he said.

He led Alexa up the stairs and through the tunnel to Underground Atlanta. He guided her along Lower Pryor Street past the vendors' carts, past Madame Zara, the fortune teller, past Johnny Rocket's, and out to Coca-Cola Plaza.

Across Martin Luther King Boulevard from Coca-Cola Plaza was the Christian Cathedral World Church. Claude pushed open a side door and drew Alexa inside.

"We go sit in the confession booth over there until that cop chasing us has given up."

"Waters, if there's a hell, you'll end up there. Don't you have a conscience? How can you hide in a cathedral?"

"You want to know why? You'll have to tell my story—that's why you're here. Miss Mason, I realize you're my last hope for getting my message out. I've thought hard about it and I'm being honest now. I probably shouldn't have killed Muhammad, but he wouldn't have helped me. So I got frustrated. I got pissed off. I also realized I'd never convince him. But I think I can convince you."

Alexa debated whether to argue with him further, knowing the weakness of his impulse control. "Go ahead and try. I'm curious."

"You already know part of this. A black man killed my parents. I was eight years old. Afterward, I went to live with my uncle. You know what that whole thing taught me? It taught me that America is evil. Our government gives handouts to these lazy, shiftless niggers, permits abortion, and discourages hard work. Those policies create an evil society, a society in which people think what's in it for me and screw everyone else.

"What about O. J. Simpson? He was acquitted because he was a nigger and they had a nigger jury. That trial was a sign of how bad things had gotten. America needs to learn the importance, the vital necessity of real Christian values, white Christian values, like hard work and respect. Now we have a black president who wasn't even born here. The first step is getting rid of all the niggers."

Alexa listened intently. Knowing how unstable and easily angered Claude was, she dared not interrupt or argue.

"I was born in Robbinsville, North Carolina. When I was eight, my mother was pregnant again and my father was taking her to the hospital. They got hit by a logging truck just as they pulled out of the driveway. But I already told you that. At least, they didn't suffer. Nigger was driving the truck.

"My sister Joanne and I went to go live with my Uncle John in Burnsville. At first, I could tell my uncle didn't want kids in the house, but I guess I grew on him. He was the one that made me see how much that nigger took from me.

"At first, I really missed my parents, especially my mom. She used to hug both me and Joanne a lot. Aunt Janice never hugged us—if she did, I can't remember. The only time my uncle hugged me was in 1979. I'll tell you about it.

"Fall of '79," he continued, "Uncle John got me up early, and we drove two hours to Greensboro. He asked me if I knew why we were there. Of course, I had no idea; I was just a boy. He told me the niggers and Jews were having a rally in Greensboro. He told me they were there to challenge God-fearing Christian Americans. We joined a caravan of other cars and trucks, and we drove through the group of protestors. Then we parked the truck, and he took me behind a large building near the square in the middle of town. It was the first time I'd seen a Klansman. There were probably a hundred Klansmen there, all decked out in their white robes. For the first time, Uncle John looked happy. He said the Klan was there to put a stop to the government handouts the niggers were getting. I remember what he said. 'Claude, was a nigger killed you mom and dad. Why should niggers deserve anything? Don't you miss your parents? Don't you want revenge?'

"He went on about it, and I decided I really did want revenge. At first, I wasn't sure, but Uncle John was right. If it weren't for that nigger, I'd still have my family. I told him so. That was when he hugged me.

"We waited around a bit. Then a cop on a motorcycle came and told us that the cops were all going to lunch. My uncle took me over to a car, and we drove back to the church where we'd seen the protestors. In the trunk was a pile of rifles and shotguns. The car in front of us stopped. We got out, and he handed me a shotgun and told everyone that I should have the first shot because a nigger killed my parents.

"There were five or six niggers coming toward us. My uncle told me to shoot the nigger in front—and I did. Then everyone started shooting, and the marchers ran. I remember how that nigger in front went down. His glasses flew up in the air.

"We got out of there pretty quick after that because my uncle said he didn't know how long the cops would stay away. It felt good to shoot that nigger. I knew it wouldn't bring my mom and dad back, but revenge is satisfying in another way. I told my uncle how it felt. He told me he was proud of me. He said I handled myself like a man. He told me the nigger who killed my parents got off scot-free. This was my payback, he told me. My uncle was a great man. He showed me how I should feel and what to do about it. So, I been killing niggers ever since. What I'm doing now, though, is more important. I'm trying to purify America."

When the train had gone by, Bud leaped across the tracks and ran along a concrete slab next to the tracks. He could see the Five Points Station ahead.

Where could they have gone? he wondered. *If it were me, I'd get out of the tunnels as quickly as I could.*

Bud ran to the platform of the Five Points Station, and on his way up the stairs to Peachtree Street, his cell phone went off.

"Bud, this is Roscoe. I couldn't do much when I got into the office. Still moving slow. But I got our ballistics guys together with the Atlanta city planners and figured out the shots that killed those cops came from the tower of the World Church Cathedral. You know, on the corner of MLK and Peachtree Center Avenue, across from Coke Plaza."

"Yeah, Roscoe, I know that cathedral. Look, that skinhead, Claude Waters—I interviewed him at the foundry—well, he's got Alexa. I chased them on foot along the MARTA tracks. I'm at the Five Points Station right now near that cathedral. You think maybe he could be in the cathedral?"

"You might as well check."

"Later, Roscoe. Thanks."

"So wasn't losing your parents just a sad, unfortunate accident? It could have been a white man driving that truck. Why do you think it has anything to do with race?" Alexa asked Claude.

"Why should I believe it has nothing to do with race?" he retorted.

"Because your uncle was a racist and he had his own agenda that included poisoning your mind. I feel sorry for you."

"Ms. Mason, I don't want or need your pity. How can I make you understand? My uncle was a great man. I've got to ensure his legacy. It was his way, his ideas of purity and grace, his fear that our Christian blood was slowly but surely being bastardized by the niggers, that they would sap all our power and dilute our heritage.

"But I know I'm not the spokesman. I know what I am and how my appearance takes away my credibility. Who's going to listen to me?

"But Ms. Mason, you've got the credibility I need. Muhammad had credibility in spades, if you'll pardon a bad pun. But he'd never have been convinced. The first thing he told me was that the races should live together. How was I to figure—guy named Muhammad? I figured he was like that Farrakhan, hated whites and would jump at the chance to achieve segregation.

"But no, Muhammad had to be preaching tolerance. That was the problem. He wasn't your run-of-the-mill uppity nigger. So, in a way, it really didn't matter that I killed him. Like he said, I couldn't have trusted him to say the right thing anyway. I ain't as dumb as he thought I was. That was his big mistake, underestimating me. You don't underestimate me, do you, Miss Mason?

"Yeah, now that I'm thinking about it," Waters rambled on, "maybe the rest of the niggers will make him a martyr, and that's good because then there'll be an even greater divide between the races. We will have segregation here one day. We'll either kill all the niggers or ship 'em back to Africa. I don't know which. It may take generations, and it has to start somewhere. I'm proud to be a part in it.

"Enough people know what I did—including you—so I'll also be a martyr. I'll be a champion of those who want to keep the white race pure. By putting that dirt in the playgrounds, I was also killing niggers. It was clever 'cuz I used their own tendencies against them. The dumber a nigger is, the more likely to die young—you know gangs an' shit. I figger if I could make 'em dumber, their own nature would do the rest. Why else do you think I did it?"

Alexa just stared at him and shuddered at the depth of the man's evil.

"You know," said Claude, proud and oblivious, "I won't be the last one. Other men who believe in a pure white America will take a lead from me. If you know, which you do now, then the facts will come out and there'll be others. That'll be my legacy."

The door of the cathedral creaked on its hinges, and Alexa heard someone enter. Instantly, she felt Claude slide a hand over her mouth and the coldness of a gun barrel against her head.

Bud walked along each row of pews. There were myriad places to hide. As he passed a confessional, a stifled cry came from within. Bud drew his gun and flung open the curtain.

Inside, Waters held Alexa with his hand over her mouth and a gun to her head.

"Let her go," Bud commanded.

"Hah! I don't think so. She's my ticket out of here."

"Take me and let her go."

"No way. As a hostage, she's a lot easier to handle than you would be. Plus, Miss Mason's been on TV. The whole country knows who she is. She's got a lot more value as a hostage than some no-name cop."

Waters's logic was irrefutable, so Bud tried a different tack.

"Let her go, Waters, and give yourself up. It'll go a lot easier for you if you start to cooperate."

"You can't be serious." Waters laughed at him. "No way I'll give myself up. If I have to kill you, I will."

"Waters, there are ten FBI agents on their way here now. You won't walk out of her alive. Whatever happens today, you'll never be able to stop running. Eventually you'll be caught. It's only a matter of time. Then your trial will be a mere formality before they fry your sorry ass."

"What's your name, cop?"

"I'm Sergeant Bud Prior."

"Not Agent Prior? I thought you said FBI."

"I'm on detail, not that it matters."

"Whatever. Maybe I'll just kill her and you. Then the FBI'll just have to try and catch me," Waters taunted him. "I have plans for Ms. Mason, and they don't include you."

Waters stood and pulled Alexa up with him. He pushed her forward and out of the confessional. As they passed the curtain that served as the door of the confessional, Alexa grabbed its edge and yanked hard, trapping both Waters's hand and the gun, and pulling the barrel away from her head. In the same motion, she stomped down hard on Waters's instep, and Bud saw his eyes widen with the sudden pain.

Bud saw Waters's gun snake out of the curtain and, almost without thinking, shot toward it. The gun dropped from Waters's bloody hand and, as quick as thought, Alexa kicked it away across the stone floor. She stomped on Waters's foot again and dove away from her captor.

Bud saw another chance and shot Waters's in the kneecap. The skinhead went down, clutching his knee, howling with pain.

"Oh, Bud!" Alexa flung her arms around Bud's neck. "I knew you'd find me. I knew you'd come." She started to kiss him, but Bud broke it off, realizing that Waters's might still be dangerous.

"Alexa, I've got to deal with Waters."

Bud rolled the skinhead over so that he was face down. He moaned as his shattered kneecap met the stone floor. Bud cuffed Waters's hands behind his back. The man's right middle finger was a bloody stump.

Bud then used his extra set of cuffs to shackle his prisoner's legs. Then he pulled out his cell phone and called Roscoe.

"I found Waters in the cathedral. He had Alexa Mason as a hostage. Waters is secure, but I need help bringing him in. Both myself and the hostage are unharmed. Waters is alive, but he'll need an ambulance."

"That's great news, Bud. I'll be over with three agents. Will that be enough?"

"Should be. I don't think he can walk."

"We're on our way."

That evening, after Alexa had made her statement to the FBI, Bud gave her a ride back to her car. He pulled his truck up behind her Corolla, still parked in front of the Summerhill Primitive Baptist Missionary Tabernacle, and walked around to hold the door for her.

She got out of his truck, flung her arms around his neck, and kissed him.

"Oh, Bud! I was so scared. You saved me. I thought I loved you before this, but now I know I love you."

"I was so frightened for you, Alexa. I know I love you too."

They kissed him again, and she pressed her slender body against his. Bud felt his heart swell with hope and promise and passion. When he opened his eyes, the sky was vivid with a magnificent sunset.

Chapter 30

Choose a Martyr

Monday, October 30

Alexa stayed at Bud's that night. She did not want to be alone. She read Christopher a bedtime story, and when the boy was asleep, she curled up in bed with Bud. She and Bud held each other in bed for a long time. Finally, Alexa spoke.

"Bud, I can't tell anyone about Waters's ideas. He wanted to get together with a Nation of Islam type. He figured Muslims would want segregation, like Farrakhan. He killed Akbar in a fit of rage, but I think he also saw Akbar as expendable. Unlike Farrakhan, Akbar wanted the races to settle their differences and live together. I think Waters was frustrated by Akbar's support of integration. Waters wanted whites to kill black people or ship them all back to Africa. I think he figured that if he got a black leader to buy into the idea . . ."

"But Alexa, that's a ridiculous idea. Think of all the wealthy black people in Atlanta, let alone other cities. They own homes and businesses. Why on earth would they choose to leave all that to move to Africa—to the third world?"

"Bud, of course it wouldn't work, but Waters wants to be a martyr for all racists. He wants to be a role model and rallying point for every stinking white supremacist in this country. He told me that removing blacks from America had to start somewhere and that he was proud to have it start with him."

Alexa held Bud tighter and whispered in his ear.

"Bud, I'm not going to let the racists have him as a martyr. I'm not going to tell his story. He's going to be forgotten as just another no-name redneck."

"Alexa, you gave the FBI statement under oath."

"But I didn't lie. I just didn't broadcast his ideas—and I won't. I just won't do it."

"Alexa, how can I know that you still don't have something material for the FBI, something that could lead to other arrests?"

"Because I'm telling you right now. You saved me. I'll always love you and trust you. The thing is, I don't know that you'll have control of any formal statement I make. Today you videotaped me, and I'm sure there'll be a written transcript. Anything like that is sure to find its way to the media, and then . . . it'll get out.

"Waters talked to me at length about his ideas. After he killed Akbar, I was scared to challenge him. He also talked about what else he had done. He told me he was at the Greensboro massacre in 1979, as a boy. He told me he fired the shot that started that whole thing. He wanted to convince me that black people were responsible for all the problems in this country. He wanted an ally to tell his story. He knew I'd have a lot more credibility than he would, and that's why he wanted me. If he had convinced me, he would have had a believable spokesperson. The one small detail he forgot was that his ideas were crap!"

"How much can you tell me, Alexa?"

"Bud, you have to keep this to yourself. Otherwise, Waters will become the hero of every stinking racist in this country. Think of the evil this one man perpetrated with that fill dirt. Suppose there were fifty people doing the same thing, a hundred, all over the country. Waters wanted me to tell his story. I won't do it. If you want me in jail rather than in your bed, then you can turn me in for not making a full statement."

"But Alexa—"

"Tell me I'm wrong, Bud. Tell me you'll have complete control of this information."

"You know I won't have complete control. Roscoe will be involved and other agents—"

"Then, no, you cannot use Waterss' story. If you ever do, I'll know I can't trust you. Then we'll have a problem."

Alexa kissed him tenderly before continuing.

"Bud, I didn't know there'd be this much negotiation about being in love, but this is new territory for me, maybe for you too. Isn't it enough that Waters has been apprehended? Waters will try to make a statement, but he has no credibility and no one will believe him. That's the way it should be. He knew he wouldn't be believable. That's why he kidnapped Akbar and me—to be his mouthpieces."

Alexa paused a moment and started softly crying.

"Bud, I know Akbar loved me. We spent an evening talking just after he arrived in Atlanta. He was so gentle and courtly while he was alive. What a loss! He's the one whose story should get out. He wanted harmony and peace between the races. He wanted all people to see each other as human beings rather than black people or white people. If a martyr comes out of this whole thing, it should be Akbar."

She started sobbing then, great heaving sobs. Bud said nothing else, just held her until she fell asleep.

CHAPTER 31

HOW IT WENT DOWN

Monday, November 7

When Bud arrived at the office on the following Monday morning, Melanie Groover was waiting for him. Jimmy Ray was with her.

"Sergeant Prior, Jimmy Ray wants to talk to you. I bailed him out of jail, and he knows he's got to do some time. I told him he'd never see the girls again unless he owned up to what he did. He's decided to be a man about it. He knows he can teach our girls a great lesson about right and wrong."

Bud looked at Jimmy Ray. His eyes were reddened, and his lower lip trembled occasionally. Rolling over on the rest of the Klan would be tough, but it was obvious Jimmy Ray had made his choice. This would be a difficult interview for him, but Bud had no doubt that he would spill his guts.

"Ms. Groover, we'll have to question Jimmy Ray without you present."

"I understand," she answered. "You know what you have to do, Jimmy Ray. The girls and I will be waiting for you."

Bud led Jimmy Ray along the hall to an interrogation room with a video camera already set up.

"Wait here, Mr. Groover. I'm going to get my partner."

Bud fetched Roscoe from his office, and the two of them sat across the table from Jimmy Ray.

"This is Sergeant Bud Prior and Special Agent Roscoe Harriman interviewing Mr. James Ray Groover on November 7. Mr. Groover, I know you have a statement to make. Why don't you start at the beginning."

"Well, my daddy was in the Klan and he told me that one day I should also join. I wasn't too sure. Especially after I met Melanie in high school. One thing I figured out is that I sure do love her. I guess that's pretty obvious.

"I stayed away from the Klan in high school after I met Melanie. Things were tough after we got married, I got into debt, and the Klan were the only folks I could go to for money.

"I had a couple of breeding pit bulls. Kept 'em in my yard. They were actually pretty gentle. Butch was just full of mischief. He was a honey and black brindle. God, he was a beautiful dog!

"One day, Butch got off his run and went down the road to the Travis place. Travis had two girls. I know those girls liked to devil Butch. Rachel and Kelly, that was their names. They was twins—looked exactly alike. Travis told me afterward that his girls was throwin' rocks at Butch. No wonder he chased 'em. They were running, just egging Butch on. Travis said he tried to bite one of them just as they got to their house. What the hell did those girls expect? They shouldn't have been throwing rocks at Butch.

"Anyway, Walter Travis sued me for assault. He got a judgment of five thousand dollars. About a week later, I lost my job at the landfill. That was when I went to the Klan for help. It was the advice of my dad.

"When I went to my first Klan meeting—I guess it was my initiation—a really weird thing happened. We was in this clearing out in the woods. You'd have to know how to get there. Well, sir, just out of the blue, this black fella comes walkin' into our meetin'. He weren't no country nigger what knew his place. No, he was an uppity city nigger. Willard Shadix who owned the drug store in Cedartown was the Grand Dragon of the Cedartown Klavern. He put a gun to that nigger's head and told him to stay put, that he weren't goin' nowhere. I remember the nigger was wearin' a yellow shirt, the kind with buttons on the collar."

Jimmy Ray paused. "Hey, could I have some water?"

"I'll get it," said Roscoe. "I won't mind missing any more N-words from the cracker."

"Look," said Jimmy Ray when Roscoe left the room. "If I rat out the Klan, what's gonna happen to me? I can't be in prison with those guys. They'll kill me."

"Well, what sort of crimes did you do? I can't help you if you murdered someone."

"I didn't do nothin'. All I did was what Waters told me. I drove the dump truck carrying dirt away from the foundry. I grabbed the girl and that Akbar fella at the rally, but Waters told me to do that. That's it. I'm tellin' you about this meeting because it seemed to lead up to everything else. Will I have to go to prison?" Jimmy Ray's voice was hoarse with emotion.

"You'll have to testify against Waters, and you'll do some time. Likely you'll not be in the general population. There is no deal without your testimony in court."

Roscoe came back into the room and handed Jimmy Ray a cup of water.

"Go ahead with your story, Mr. Groover," said Bud. "We'll talk about the rest of it later."

"No, sir, I need to know now. I'm gonna give up some guys, and I need to get something out of it. I heard about your witness protection plan. That's what I want—a new start in a new town when I get out. You'll set me up with a job too and make sure my wife and kids are protected."

"What sort of crimes?" asked Roscoe. "Rolling over on Claude Waters won't help you. We already got enough on him to put him away for a hundred years."

"Not about Waters. I know about a murder, but you gotta get me into that witness protection thing first."

"Look, Jimmy Ray," said Bud, "it's complicated. Roscoe, have we ever done this for hate crimes?"

"No," answered Roscoe, "it's pretty much for mob-related stuff. Look, you cracker shithead, if you want any chance at all of seeing daylight again in your lifetime, you tell us what you know. When did this murder happen?"

Roscoe must be really angry, thought Bud. *He doesn't usually talk like that.*

"Not that long ago," continued Jimmy Ray. "It was the city black fella I told you about. Shadix killed him. I saw it. Frank Tyson and Johnnie Veal helped him. I'll roll on them too. Once the nigger knew he was done for, he started sweating, looked like a chocolate bar melting in the sun. I told that to Willard. He said the nigger looked more like a piece of shit with legs."

There was a hard edge of desperation in Jimmy Ray's voice. He was giving up the other Klansmen with no guarantee of immunity—throwing himself on their mercy.

"I told the rest of them that we should just let the nigger go. He wanted to be on his way too, backing out of the clearing real slow like he was walking away from a mean dog. He talked like a white man too, not like a Cedartown jigaboo. I recall what he said: 'If you gentlemen don't mind, I'd just as soon be on my way.'

"Then Veal and Tyson grabbed him and tied him to a tree and then we lit a cross. Once we lit that cross, the nigger pissed himself, he was so scared. I could smell it.

"Then we all put on our Klan robes and hoods and swore an oath about sending the niggers back to Africa an' purifyin' America. Then Willard told Johnny Veal to rough him up a bit. Veal kicked him and punched up pretty good. Willard stopped him before the nigger got unconscious. Then Willard took out his knife and slit the nigger's throat. He hit a squirter, and blood got sprayed all over us. We all watched him bleed to death. We all got blood on our robes.

"When the nigger had bled out, we took his body to the old landfill. They knew I worked there. They made me bury him with the D-9. Even though I'd lost my job there, I still had an extra key to the D-9."

"Wait," said Bud. "Excuse us for a second."

Bud pulled Roscoe outside. "Did we just solve Jack Williams's murder?"

"I think we did, Bud." Roscoe said grimly. "With this Groover's testimony, Williams's murder is a hate crime and we can keep the case federal. If he testifies, I think we should give him some sort of immunity. He'll still have to do some time on the kidnapping thing. Getting Williams's killers is pretty big."

"Roscoe, I don't want you to think I'm getting soft, but is there something we can do for his wife and kids?"

"Bud, he's gonna have to do some time as an accessory. If the federal prosecutor is sympathetic to the wife's situation, then maybe. Maybe the judge will cut him some slack because he cooperated with us. However, he's not a great witness—not that much credibility."

"Roscoe, it's for his wife. She gave me the first lead that let me find Alexa. God knows, she deserves better than him, but she loves him, or says she does. She has no job skills. I've talked to her, and she trusts me. She's committed to raising her daughters to be good human beings—with or without Jimmy Ray. You know, he wouldn't even be here without her threatening to leave him. I told him he'd do some time, but I wasn't sure we could put him in the general population."

"You make a good point, Bud. I don't think he's suffered enough. A few years inside in isolation will give him some time to ponder. If he testifies and goes into gen pop, he'll be dead in less than a day. He'll have to do his time in solitary. If he wants to get back to his family, which honestly seems a stretch to me, then he'll spend that time alone."

They went back into the interrogation room, and Bud asked Jimmy Ray to spell the names of the three other men.

"I'll even write 'em down for you," said Jimmy Ray. Bud got him a legal pad and pen.

"Wanna hear how I met Waters?" Jimmy Ray asked when he was finished writing. "Johnny Veal told me that all the backhoe guys in Atlanta would meet up at a bar in Atlanta—a titty bar, you know. It's called Mama Gloria's."

"That's on Fulton Industrial, isn't it?" asked Roscoe.

"That's the one."

"Bud, we've staked it out before."

"Don't tell my wife I was in there, okay?" pleaded Jimmy Ray. "I got enough shit to deal with. I am helpin' you guys, ain't I?"

"Go ahead with your story," said Bud.

"I went there with Veal and Tyson. They knew one of the girls. Her name was Delores. We was drinkin' Southern Comfort. I remember we was celebratin' 'cause Veal just sold his dune buggy, so he was buyin'. We were on the third round, feelin' no pain, when that skinhead Waters walked in the joint.

"He sat at the table next to us. Scary fuckin' dude. Skinny as a fuckin' rail. He was wearing all black. His T-shirt said Shit Happens. He was drinkin' shots of tequila with a beer chaser. Delores was smiling at Waters all the way through her dance.

"Veal was pretty drunk. He stood up and yelled at Delores—something about how she needed a real man.

"Waters was up in Veal's face in a second, telling him to show respect. Well, Veal gets pretty mean when he's drunk. 'Why should I respect these whores?' he said to Waters. 'Because they're white,' Waters replied. Veal sat down and shut up at that point. Veal's pretty big, about 280. They were interested in him playin' football at Georgia, but his SATs weren't good enough. Most guys back off when they see how big he is. Not Waters. I had the feelin' Waters could have clocked him any time. I could see that Waters scared Veal.

"Then Waters got all friendly and asked us if any of us had any experience with a backhoe. I jumped on that. I told him I jus' got fired from a job and they hired a nigger in my place.

"'A lot of us got problems with niggers,' was what Waters said. 'Well, sure, don't we all?' Tyson answered him.

"Then Waters said he needed a good backhoe man, and he looked at me. Then Waters talked about how we should be dumping hazardous waste on niggers. He told us how Germany wanted to send a shipload of hazardous waste to Africa, but those bleeding hearts in the UN wouldn't let them. He went on and on about what a great idea that was. Then he asked if he could talk to me outside about the backhoe work. We went outside, and he told me he was working at the foundry and needed a backhoe man on his crew. He asked if I could drive a truck. Well, I can drive 'bout anything with wheels, and that's what I told him.

"He asked if I had any HazMat training. I told him no. He said not to worry; he'd get me the papers I needed. He gave me a card with a couple of numbers on it and told me to be at the foundry the next morning. He gave me directions.

"So I started at Seitzman's Foundry the next day. First thing, Waters introduces me to this really odd dude. His name was Face. I asked him how he got a name like that. He told me his given name was Segovia, but that everyone called him Face because he was such a handsome dude. He had blond hair and a long ponytail. Waters said Face knew the ropes and would tell me what to do. Waters then told me he had a plan to take the dirt from the foundry and give it away as fill dirt. I don't know what he meant. Last thing he said was that he liked the idea of using a mess created by a Jew to poison niggers.

"Anyway, Face had me jump up on the backhoe and load a dump truck with some dirt. There was a big pile of dirt at the foundry sittin' out on a big plastic sheet. That was the dirt we used.

"When we had the truck full, Waters told us to take it to a church near Mama Gloria's and dump it where they told us. Face knew the way. We got to this church in an all-black neighborhood. I can tell you I was scared. I mean, two white boys sure had no business in that part of town. Face knocked on the door of the church, and this ol' preacher came out. He seemed real glad to see us, even if we was white. The preacher showed us where to dump the dirt. Face asked him if he wanted it raked out smooth, that we could do that too. The preacher said that'd be real nice. So that's what we did. Only took an hour or so to spread the dirt around and rake it out. When we was done, Face asked if I wanted to catch a quick beer at Mama Gloria's. I asked him if Waters would mind. He told me no, that Waters expected him to have a beer. Face paid for the beer and then bought us each a girl for a half hour. Then we drove back to the foundry.

"Look, you won't tell my wife about that part, will you?" asked Jimmy Ray.

"No, we won't tell her," said Bud. "Being an unfaithful husband and a complete scumbag is still not a crime according to the FBI."

"On the trip back, Face told me how much he liked working for Waters and how much he hated niggers. His mother had a nigger pimp, he told me. The pimp sometimes hit him. That was why Face hated niggers. He told me his mother was really stupid, that she was a nigger lover and had been all her life. Face told me he was just plumb lucky he wasn't a nigger. He said his mother fucked plenty of niggers. Face's mother gave him this really terrible name—Segovia Lavoris Chism. He said 'Chism' was supposed to sound like 'gism,' you know, sperm. He said his mother heard the other two words on the radio. He said it was a nigger name and he was just as happy bein' called Face.

"I asked him what his mother's name was. He told me she didn't have a real name, just a whore name. She went by Honey Dew Melon. He told me it was because she had really big tits."

"You were telling us about the fill dirt, Mr. Groover," Roscoe prompted.

"Oh, yeah. Then that woman, the one we kidnapped, got in the papers sayin' that the niggers was being poisoned. Once we knew that march was gonna happen, Claude said he had plans for me and Face. We all met in the parking lot of the old stadium, you know, before they built Turner Field. There were about three hundred Klan there and about four hundred cops. The cops were letting people gather, but they weren't happy about it.

"Coupla guys in a car got really pissed off at a cop. This cop was a nigger. Man, he was huge. Probably went three hundred pounds. These two guys pull up in an old Chevy with a Stars'n'Bars decal on the windshield. Tennessee plates, if I recall. The two guys were really drunk, and they had a pair of pit bulls and four cases of beer in the backseat. I noticed them 'cause I thought it was kinda mean to keep those dogs in the backseat all the way from Tennessee.

"Anyway, Waters told us some of the cops would be shot during the rally. He gave us real specific instructions—"

"Wait! Did Waters shoot those cops?" asked Bud.

"I don't know, man. Probably. Face and I were supposed to go in with the Klan, and as soon as things heated up, we had to drop our robes, grab the woman who was speaking, grab that guy Muhammad as well, and carry them off. We used Waters's car and left it near the old police station on Piedmont where we could get to it easily.

"By the way, I saw that woman in Mama Gloria's one night before the rally. Waters met us there after we dumped some soil at night and parked the truck. She seemed way too high class for that place. Waters somehow got her to sit with us and have a drink. I could see she was real nervous. She said she had to make a call and ran out. Jumped up so quick, she dumped a drink in Waters's lap. He was pissed about it."

"Back to the rally," said Roscoe.

"Oh, yeah. So we marched up with the Klan. Then those two cops got shot. I have no idea how that happened. Like I said, maybe Waters did it, but I don't know. The plan was that once the shooting started, Face and me grab the girl and the nigger and hightail it up to Marietta. Waters was gonna meet up with us later.

"So that's what we did. We took them up to Marietta and stayed in a trailer with that whore . . . well, you know. You saw us there."

Chapter 32

Where to, Mister?

Friday December 15

Alexa had spent Thanksgiving with Bud and Christopher. They all had a wonderful time. She felt lucky to be alive after her kidnapping, and Bud had spared no part of himself in the effort to save her. But since then, Bud seemed content with letting their relationship coast, and it troubled her.

How could I not love him? she thought as they were seated at a booth at La Tavola, an Italian place in Virginia-Highlands with a stellar wine list. Bud had asked her to dinner with him, and Alexa was hoping that tonight her relationship with Bud would progress.

"This wine is really good, Bud."

"Yeah, I don't really know much about wine, but I keep trying different ones when there's an opportunity."

"I don't want to get too serious before dinner," Alexa began, "but I need to know where things are going with us. You've been so wonderful and sweet to me, but you don't seem to want any sort of commitment."

"Well, I didn't want to rush you."

"Bud, two people cannot go through an experience such as we had without falling in love. Don't you want me to be with you?"

"I do," he agreed.

"You didn't hesitate when it came to saving me from Waters. Was that just part of your job? Bud, I can't keep wondering. You need to fish or cut bait. I love you, and I love your son. But that's not enough, as you well know. Where is this going?"

"You never did mince words, Alexa."

"Right now's the opportunity, Bud Prior." Her tone was vehement.

"Look, Alexa." He stared at her for a long moment and touched the back of her hand. "God, you're so beautiful, but I'm frightened of what could happen."

"What do you mean, Bud?"

Alexa watched him turn his wine glass slowly as he struggled to tell her. When he looked up at her, his eyes were moist.

"All the women I love seem to die. I couldn't stand it if that happened to you. Sandy, my wife, died from leukemia. I loved her, but I could have been a better husband. I feel like I disappointed her in so many ways. I carry that guilt, like maybe her getting ill was my fault."

"How can you say that, Bud? You were just unlucky."

"Sandi's not the only one."

"What do you mean?"

"Alexa, I said I could have been a better husband. My heart wasn't always with Sandi. I fell in love with someone else when Sandi was pregnant with Christopher. What sort of man does that?"

"Bud—" she began, but he held up a hand to stop her.

"There's more, Alexa. I've never told anyone this, and I want to tell you."

Again, he slowly turned his wine glass, taking care, it seemed to Alexa, to keep the base in exactly the same spot on the tablecloth.

"The woman I fell in love with was another cop. I met her during an investigation. She was killed because we were together."

"Bud, no one is perfect. Please let this go, for our sake. How many years have you been carrying this guilt? I'm not judging you. I never will. Put it down—for our sake."

"Alexa, I'm trying to, but I felt so guilty when Sandi became ill. It was as if God were punishing me by . . . by killing off the women I loved."

"Oh, Bud, I'm so sorry. This may sound like a cliché, but we all have history, and we all have baggage. That's how we learn to live as human beings. It's not easy. It's not supposed to be.

"When I first moved to Atlanta," she continued, "and had just started my company, I was still working out of my apartment. I was twenty-nine and worried about turning thirty. More than once, I brought a man home from a bar with me. I liked the sense of danger and abandon. The last time I did that, I met a block mason in a bar just round the corner from here. His arms were the size of most men's legs. He had rattlesnakes tattooed on both forearms. It was such a rush because he seemed so dangerous. He was rough with me sexually, and living dangerously became no longer fun because I realized what could happen. The man was gone the next morning, and I felt relieved because I knew I had nothing to say to him, that all he was was a stranger I wanted to fuck. I felt humiliated to be such a slave to my lust."

She touched his hand.

"But I still love a pirate, and, Bud, part of you is a pirate too. That's one of the reasons I love you."

"But, Alexa, all the women I love die young. I couldn't stand it if you—"

"Not me, Bud, and the proof is I didn't die. You saved me. You've lost that jinx! When are you going to realize it?"

He stared at the wineglass for a long moment and then touched her hand.

"I'm still selfish," Bud whispered. "I can't put my heart in such jeopardy ever again."

"Bud, I fell in love with you because you are kind and considerate and tender. The way you've parented Christopher shows how kind you are. The man you are today is because of your history. You're a pirate and a dangerous man, but you're also a sweet, kind, and tender man. I couldn't help but fall in love with the total package."

She took a sip of wine before continuing. "Bud, none of us have any guarantee how long we'll live. Don't you want to be together now?"

"Yes, but—"

"There are no 'buts.' The question is, where to, mister? And I need an answer."

CPSIA information can be obtained at www.ICGtesting.com
Printed in the USA
LVOW071312030312